To Jaime Steinman-Jones and Kerissa Blake

DEFY

SINNERS OF SAINT

L.J. SHEN

Defy
Edited by: Karen Dale Harris, Ellie McLove
Cover Designer: Letitia Hasser, RBA Designs
Interior Formatting: Stacey Blake, Champagne Formats

"I would always rather be happy than dignified."
—Charlotte Brontë, *Jane Eyre*

Soundtrack

"Secretly"—Skunk Anansie

"R U Mine?"—Arctic Monkeys

"Under Your Spell"—Desire

"Colors"—Halsey

"Crazy In Love"—Nightcore

"Whistle for the Choir"—The Fratellis

"Halo"—Texas

"Atomic"—Blondie

Originally, the anchor symbol was not used by those on the water, but by people on land. During the early years of Christianity, Christians were under heavy persecution by the Romans. To show their religion to other practicing Christians under the watchful eye of the ruling people, they would wear anchor jewelry or even tattoo anchors on themselves. The anchor was seen as a symbol of strength as anchors hold down ships even in the stormiest of weather. It was also a popular symbol because of its close resemblance to the cross. Anchors were also used to mark safe houses for those seeking refuge from persecution.

MyNameNecklace.com

My name is Melody Greene, and I have a confession to make.
I slept with my student, a senior in high school.
Multiple times.
I had multiple orgasms.
In multiple positions.
I slept with my student and I enjoyed it.
I slept with my student, and I'd do it all over again if I could turn back time.

My name is Melody Greene, and I got kicked out of my position as a teacher and did my walk of shame à la Cersei Lannister from the principal's office, minutes after said principal threatened to call the cops on me.
My name is Melody Greene, and I did something bad because it made me feel good.
Here is why it was totally worth it.

Chapter One

I snailed my way out of the principal's office toward the SoCal mid-winter clouds. Anger, humiliation, and self-loathing coated every inch of my soul, creating a film of desperation I was desperate to scratch away.

Rock. Meet. Bottom.

I'd just found out All Saints High was not going to renew my contract as a teacher next year unless I pulled my shit together and performed some magic that'd transform my students into attentive human beings. Principal Followhill said that I showed zero authority and that the literature classes I was teaching were falling behind. To add fuel to the fire, last week I'd received notice that I was getting kicked out of my apartment at the end of next month. The owner had decided to remodel and move back in.

Also, the sexting partner I'd bagged through a questionable dating site had just fired me a message saying he wouldn't be able to make it to our first in-person date because his mom wouldn't give him her car tonight.

He was twenty-six.

So was I.

Being picky was a luxury a woman who hadn't seen a real-life

1

cock in four years really didn't have.

And, as a matter of fact, other than a few short flings, I'd never had a relationship. At all. With anyone. Ballet had always come first. Before men and before *me*. For a while, I'd actually thought it was enough. Until it wasn't.

When did it all go wrong?

I could tell you when—right after I started college. Eight years ago, I got accepted to Julliard and was about to fulfill my dream to become a professional ballerina. This was what I'd worked for my whole life. My parents had taken out loans to pay my way through dancing competitions. Boyfriends were deemed an unwelcome distraction, and my only focus was joining a prestigious New York or European ballet company and becoming a prima ballerina.

Dancing was my oxygen.

When I said my goodbyes to my family and waved at them from the security point at the airport, they told me to break a leg. Three weeks into my first semester at Julliard, I literally did. Broke it in a freakish escalator accident on my way down to the subway.

It not only killed my career dreams and lifelong plan, but also sent me packing and back to SoCal. After a year of sulking, feeling sorry for myself and developing a steady relationship with my first (and last) boyfriend—a dude named Jack Daniels—my parents convinced me to pursue a career in teaching. My mom was a teacher. My dad was a teacher. My older brother was a teacher. They loved teaching.

I *hated* teaching.

This was my third year of teaching, and my first—and judging by my performance, only—year at All Saints High in Todos Santos, California. Principal Followhill was one of the most influential women in town. Her polished bitchery was formidable. And she absolutely despised me from the get-go. My days under her reign were numbered.

As I approached my twelve-year-old Ford Focus parked across the aisle from her Lexus and her son's monstrous Range Rover (Yeah, she'd bought her son, a senior, a fucking luxury SUV. Why would an eighteen-year-old need a car so big? Maybe so it could accommodate his giant-ass ego?), I decided my situation couldn't possibly get any worse.

But I was wrong.

I slid into my car and started backing up into the almost empty parking lot, slipping back toward the two pricey symbols of a small dick. At the exact same moment, Mr. Living With His Mom texted me again. The green bubble flashed with **GOT THE CAR. R8DY TO SEX IT UP?** accompanied with approximately three thousand question marks.

I got distracted.

I got annoyed.

I bumped straight into Principal Followhill's son's SUV.

Choking the steering wheel and gasping in horror, I slapped my hand over my heart to make sure it didn't shoot out of my ribcage. Shit. Shit. *Shit!* The thud that filled my ears and shook my car didn't leave any room for doubt.

I'd done to his SUV what Keanu Reeves did to the movie *Dracula*. I'd fucking ruined it.

My fight-or-flight adrenalin kicked in, and I briefly contemplated whether I should hit the gas, assume an alias, and flee the country to hide in a cave somewhere in the Afghan mountains.

How was I going to pay for the damage? I had a big deductible and there was that notice at home about my last insurance premium being late. Was I even covered? Principal Followhill was going to kill me.

Mustering my courage, I peeled my sorry ass off my seat. Technically speaking, Jaime's precious black SUV wasn't supposed to be parked in the teachers' lot. Then again, Jaime Followhill got away with a lot of shit he wasn't supposed to, thanks to his looks, social status, and powerful parents.

I circled around to find my cheap car's ass that was kissing his Range Rover's back quarter panel, leaving a dent the size of Africa.

Suffice it to say, *now* things couldn't get any worse.

But I was wrong. Again.

Bending down, I squinted at the destruction, not giving a damn about the fact that my brown knee-length dress danced in the air, exposing my new lace panties. There wasn't anyone else in the parking lot to see them, and it wasn't as if I was going to be flaunting them in front of Mr. Living With His Mom tonight.

"Oh, no, no, no…" I chanted breathlessly.

I heard a guttural growl. "Next time you bend over like this, Ms. G, make sure I'm not behind you, or it'll end up on *National Geographic: When Predators Strike.*"

I slowly straightened, pushing my reading glasses up the bridge of my nose and scowling at Jaime Followhill as I took him in.

Jaime looked like the lovechild of Ryan Gosling and Channing Tatum, and I was not making this shit up. (Side note: This would be a great idea for a M/M romance novel. I'd totally read it, anyway.) Sandy-blond hair tied into a low, messy bun, indigo eyes, and the body of a male stripper. Seriously, the kid was so ripped, his guns were the size of fucking bowling balls. He was a walking, talking cliché of the prom king in a 90s movie. A baller who had every girl's attention at All Saints High…

And his eyes were now on *me* as he strode closer to his very smashed ride.

He wore a tight gray Henley shirt that made his biceps and pecs stand out, slim dark denim, and high-top shoes that looked so expensive and tasteless you just knew P Diddy had to be behind that design. He had a few bruises on his arms and a fading black eye. I knew where he'd gotten them. Rumor was he and his stupid

4

friends beat the shit out of each other on the weekends in a fight-club game they called Defy.

Guess Pretty Boy wasn't too rich to be pushed around. I wondered if his mother knew about Defy.

Wait, did he ask me a question about my hamster? Or was it my hamstrings?

"Well, fuck me to the moon and back." He stopped a few inches from our cars, releasing a wicked grin. It looked like the two cars had melded together. Like his SUV was giving birth to my ugly car through its rear end, and now the SUV's significant other (Principal Followhill's Lexus) was demanding a paternity test.

I taught Jaime, and he was one of the few kids that I could count on not to yell/scream/throw crap at people in English Lit. He wasn't a good student by any stretch of the imagination, but he was too busy with his cell phone to make trouble in my class.

"Sorry." I released a pained breath, my shoulders sagging in defeat.

He lifted the hem of his shirt and rubbed his perfect six-pack, stretching lazily and yawning at the same time. "Seems to me like I fucked your car up, Ms. Greene."

Wait…what?

"You…" I cleared my throat, looking around to make sure it wasn't a prank. "You fuck—I mean, you damaged my car?"

"Yeah. Bumped right into your ass. Pun intended, obvs." He kneeled down, frowning at the spot where our two vehicles met. He brushed his tan palm over the shiny paint of his SUV.

Jaime made it sound like he was the one who'd crashed his car into mine. I had no idea why. He wasn't even in his car. He'd just walked up. Maybe he wanted to blackmail me?

I considered myself a respectable teacher with a moral compass. But I also considered myself someone who would prefer not to bathe in the ocean and sleep in her car. That was exactly what I would need to do to survive the financial blow if I admitted to being at blame for hitting his expensive car.

"James..." I sighed, clutching onto the gold anchor necklace hanging around my neck.

He shook his head and raised his hand in the air. "So I screwed up your ride. Shit happens. Let me make it up to you."

What. The. Heck?

I didn't know what game he was playing. I just knew that he was probably better at it than I was. So, in true Melody Greene fashion, I turned around and walked straight back to my car, essentially running away from the situation like the little pussy that I was.

"Whoa, not so fast." He chuckled as he grabbed me by the elbow and spun me around.

My eyes darted to his palm on my flesh. He lowered his hand, but it was too late. Butterflies somersaulted in my stomach, and my skin prickled with need. I was hot and bothered by one of my pupils.

Only Jaime Followhill wasn't just any pupil. He was also a sex god.

There was gossip in the hallways of All Saints High to prove it, enough stories to compete with the length of the fucking Complete Works of Shakespeare. And that wasn't the only things that were long and impressive about the guy if the rumors were true.

Followhill made me almost as uncomfortable as his mother did. Only difference was his mom inspired fear in me, while he poked at my most sensitive spot. He made me feel embarrassed.

That could be because my eyes always drifted his way while I taught his Lit class. Like a moth to a flame, I always noticed him, even when I didn't want to. I was worried he knew that too. That I was looking at him in a way I shouldn't be when he was dicking around, messing with his phone.

Not like a teacher.

But like a woman.

"I said I dented your car." His blue eyes shimmered with intensity.

Why was he doing this? And why the fuck did I care? This kid received more pocket money than I had in all my savings combined. If he wanted to shoulder this, I should just accept.

Was it a better grade he was after? Doubted it. Jaime was a senior on his way out the door. I'd heard his rich ass had landed a spot at an excellent Texas university (see: Mommy Dearest), where he'd play football and probably fuck his way into some kind of a man-whore Guinness World Record.

"You did," I said, swallowing. "And right now, I'm running late. Please step out of my way."

We mentally shook hands on that lie, our eyes hard on one another. I had a feeling I was digging a hole. A hole in which I was about to dump a ton of dark shit that'd land me in hot trouble. I was striking a deal with the devil's spawn. Even though I had a good eight years on him, I knew who he was.

One of the Four HotHoles.

A self-centered, privileged princeling who ruled this town.

Jaime took another step my way, his body flush with mine. His breath skated over my face. Mint gum, aftershave, and musky male sweat that made me oddly heady. I was so unprepared for this that my face twitched.

I took a step back.

He took a step forward.

Bending his head down, he moved his lips close to mine. To my horror, my knees buckled, and I knew exactly why.

"I owe you," he murmured darkly. "And I'll make sure you get to cash in on that debt. Soon. Very soon."

"I don't need your money," I sputtered, my womb tingling with fuzzy warmth.

His mesmerizing eyes widened, and he flashed me a dimpled smirk. "It's not money I'm going to give you."

How could someone so young be so arrogant and self-assured? I felt his thumb stroking my stomach, barely touching, teasing, making me quiver through the thin fabric of my dress. It was like he'd shoved his whole fist into me and attacked my mouth with his.

I licked my lips and blinked, astonished.

Holy shit.

Holy. Fucking. Shit.

Jaime Followhill was hitting on me. Blatantly. In the parking lot. In plain sight.

I wasn't a troll. I still had a dancer's body after all, green eyes, a nice California tan, and soft chestnut curls. But I didn't exactly give the cheerleading crowd a run for their money.

Tripping backward, I swallowed a groan, feeling my pulse everywhere, eyelids included. "That's enough, James. Drive safely, and please be sure to do your homework for tomorrow," I had the audacity to say.

I tucked myself back into my Ford, and then accidentally bumped my car into the Range Rover one more time before I fled the scene, smearing the ugly dent into a long, wide scratch. From the rearview mirror, I watched as he cocked his eyebrows at me in a challenge.

I drove so fast I swore my curls transformed into a dramatic blow-out by the time I parked under my building.

At home, I slouched on my couch in front of my phone and waited for Principal Followhill to call and tell me she was firing my ass and suing me for every single penny that I had. Or in my case *didn't* have.

Long hours passed, but the call never came. I crawled into bed and closed my eyes at ten p.m. but couldn't sleep to save my life. All I thought about was that gorgeous asshole, Jaime Followhill.

How he smelled like the hottest guy I'd ever been near.

How he looked like the most delicious thing in the world when he rubbed his tan six-pack.

How he helped me out of a shitty situation without flinching, knowing that his mother would probably crush me for this, and now…*he wanted something back.*

On paper, he was still a kid, but every other part of him felt like a man this afternoon.

It so defied logic, it was unnerving, almost infuriating when I thought about it.

This morning, I'd woken up with the impression that I hated the Followhills.

But after this afternoon, there was no denying it—there was at least one Followhill I wanted to get *very* friendly with.

Chapter Two

HERE WAS ALL YOU NEEDED to know about Todos Santos: it was the richest town in California and, as a direct result, home to the most entitled teenagers in the world. My students knew I couldn't fail them. Their parents had enough power to strip me of my citizenship and banish me to an oxygen-deprived planet. These kids did whatever they wanted during class, much to no one's surprise.

The day after the car incident was different.

I taught six classes. The first five had gone better than expected, meaning I didn't have to slap anyone with a detention slip or call an ambulance/911/a SWAT team for assistance. But it was the sixth and last class that changed my life forever.

I sashayed into Jaime's class—following another barking session from his bitchy mom—into an echoing silence I wasn't used to. Everyone was seated, nobody threw anything, and Vicious, Jaime's BFF, hadn't cut anyone's face and adorned their forehead with a satanic symbol just to burn time.

Normally, this was the part where I had to contain the wrath and deplorable behavior of the Four HotHoles. (Hot Assholes, as they were dubbed by everyone in Todos Santos.) It was three months before graduation, and they were all seniors, a possible excuse for their behavior. Except they'd been this way since the first day.

There was Jaime, who spent my class texting the whole world and drawing the attention of every girl who wasn't tongue-deep into Trent Rexroth, the underprivileged mocha-skinned football star, who made out with random chicks in the back. He once had a girl sucking his cock under his table in calculus. I kid you not. There was Dean Cole, the airheaded stoner who enjoyed pranks and annoying me in equal measure, and finally, Baron "Vicious" Spencer, the World's Biggest Jerk.

Vicious was by far the worst. He made good on his name. So goddamned cold and sullen all the time that people nicknamed him after Sid Vicious of the Sex Pistols. He had coal black hair, expressionless eyes, fair skin, and the kind of rebellious anger that could electrify you to the point of the chills. The permanent tick of his clenched square jaw made girls wet their panties from fear *and* lust. He was a jock, like all the HotHoles, but he was leaner than the rest, not as muscular. But scarier. Definitely fucking scarier.

That day, Millie LeBlanc, a sweet girl who was the most frequent target of Vicious's wrath, arrived three minutes late. I tilted my head, signaling for her to take a seat. I felt bad for her. Her parents had dragged her all the way from Virginia her senior year to take a job as live-in servants at one of the town's many mansions—Vicious Spencer's house to be exact.

As always, she strode right in the psycho's direction and took the empty seat beside him as if she didn't know or care who Vicious was. My soul shouted an extended "*Noooooooo!*" when I saw how he was watching her. *He will grind you and feed you to his pet snake,* I wanted to warn.

But Emilia just lifted her head, offered a polite smile, and drawled a Southern "hey, y'all" in the direction of him and the other HotHoles. Vicious blinked slowly, intrigued by the idea that she dared to speak to him without permission, and his expression clouded into a taut frown.

"Motherfucker, did you just 'hey, y'all' me?" He let out a feral growl. "Please tell me it's a fucking safe word you're using now because some new boyfriend shoved the Confederate flag up your ass, pole included. Otherwise, don't ever fucking 'hey y'all' me again."

Wow. That was more words than he'd spoken all year.

Millie sighed and said, "I'm only trying to be polite. You should try it sometime."

"I don't do polite," he retorted, a rare smile tugging on his lips. Usually, he seemed to despise her, but he was studying her so intently it looked as if he was the one who'd like to shove numerous things up her perky little butt.

"Leave him alone, baby doll." Trent, the guy next to her (who took a breather from letting the chick next to him suck his thumb) glanced from Dean to Vicious. "Vicious stop being a—"

"A raging fucking asshole," Jaime finished from behind them, scraping his chair back and towering over their heads, his sculpted muscles flexed to the max.

Goddammit. It was the first time my workday had ever been blissfully uneventful. The HotHoles just had to ruin it.

Before I could warn everyone off with an impotent threat I'd never follow through with, Jaime galloped toward Vicious and pinned him to the nearest wall, his fingers laced firmly around Vic's neck in a death squeeze.

"Where's your loyalty, man? Leave it be, okay?" Jaime tightened his hold on Vicious's neck.

"James!" I raised my voice, flying up from my chair and banging my palm over the desk. "Back to your seat, now!"

Vicious looked thoroughly amused, rolling his head on the wall and laughing like a maniac. Jaime and Vicious were best friends, but they were also two alphas with a shitload of testoster-one and hormones coursing through their veins.

They were also the inventors of Defy. The teachers and high school staff didn't know too much about Defy, because it went on at Vicious's house parties over the weekends, but we got the general idea. The game was simple: Our students challenged each other to bloody fights and beat the shit out of each other. For fun.

Defy was supposedly voluntary, but I didn't doubt people were afraid enough of Vicious to indulge his whims, however ridiculous or dangerous.

"Make me," Jaime challenged me on a whisper, his eyes nar-rowing into slits and zeroing in on my face, his fingers still digging into the neck of an amused, bluish Vic.

Jesus Christ. I never touched Followhill when it came to deten-tions and tardy slips. His mom was the fucking principal, and she already hated my guts. But he'd cornered me. I had to react.

I clutched my necklace tighter.

Why was he doing this? Yesterday, he eye-fucked me to uncon-sciousness and back. And now…he…he…

Oh, shit. Now he's cashing in on the debt.

He didn't want me to back down. He wanted me to accept his dare. Was I going to take the bait? It wasn't like I had much choice. I owed him big time for the Range Rover. Whatever it was he want-ed from me, it was already his.

"You've just landed yourself in detention for the next week, starting this afternoon." I pulled open the drawer of my wooden desk and started filling out the detention form.

Everyone fell silent. I'd never done this before. Not to a senior and definitely not to James Charles Followhill III.

From the corner of my eye, I watched as Jaime finally let go of Vicious's neck. Vicious made a sucking sound and grabbed his junk, motioning to Jaime, laughing as he strode back to his seat.

Other students slapped his back and looked between them, slipping notes. Probably bets on an impending Defy fight that was about to go down this weekend.

I smacked the detention slip on Jaime's desk, and he jerked his eyes up, beaming a smile at me so sinister my panties melted into gooey, sweet liquid. We both knew what I was doing.

Awarding him with one-on-one time with me, exactly what he wanted.

Accepting an arrangement that'd put me in a fragile, potentially disastrous spot.

I was saying thank you to him for threatening my class, telling them to behave, so that he'd be the only person in detention for the next week.

And at this point, there was no denying it—I was allowing myself to free-fall headfirst into the end of my career, doing somersaults on my way down.

Jaime Followhill had celebrated his eighteenth birthday three days before the parking lot incident, which made the chain of recent events even more suspicious. Had he waited to hit on me? Why? He could have any girl in school. (After Trent Rexroth had a taste, of course.)

I'd already spent my lunch break roaming his Facebook page like there was no tomorrow. His timeline was a pointed reminder that he was eight years my junior. He had pictures from summer camp, for fuck's sake. He was always sporting a dimply smile, tan muscular forearms, a stunning pair of bright blues, and a ton of friends.

Jaime had everything, and I had nothing. He had a coddled

past, a cushy present, and a dazzling future. I, on the other hand, was already tainted with career failure and headed toward a life of scrambling to stay employed and out of debt. We didn't make sense. Even for a fling.

But I was too selfish and vulnerable to say no. Besides, having him would be like sticking it to his mom without really letting her know about it.

Win-win, right?

That afternoon, I slipped into the classroom where detention took place, noting that the wooden door to the room had a window.

I wasn't surprised to see the blond HotHole was already there, sitting in the front row, jingling his car keys—and our secret—between his strong fingers with a smirk, haunting me with his teal eyes. Gulping, I sat down at the teacher's table and took out my laptop and some exams I needed to grade.

"Put your phone in your backpack, Jaime." I wet my lips, my eyes focused on my paperwork.

He did as he was told, but I felt his lingering gaze licking me everywhere. My self-consciousness levels were so high I was on the verge of throwing up. I acted like I was about to commit a crime. In a way, I was.

After a few minutes of me pretending to type absolutely nothing on my laptop and him staring at me with a cocky smile, like he was about to devour me at any second, I grunted, "Why don't you do your homework? I'm sure you can do something constructive with your time while you're here." He had two hours to burn, and my face couldn't be *that* fascinating.

But I swore I heard him mumble, "Sizing up my prey is constructive."

My head bolted up from my screen, and I shot him a dirty look. "Excuse me?"

He tilted his chin up, flashing a row of pearly whites of the

Hollywood variety. "Ms. Greene, this is going to happen."

I knew what he meant.

"I have no idea what you mean," I snipped. *Pshh*. Playing games with an eighteen-year-old. I promised myself that after today, I was going to take a long, hard look at my life. Preferably while enjoying a generous glass of wine. Well, not a glass, maybe more like a bowl.

Jaime leaned forward on his elbows, his huge arms spanning his whole desk. The devious twinkle in his eyes assured me, once again, that his age was merely a number. Hell, he'd probably slept with more people than I'd *kissed* in my entire life.

"Yes, you do. You know," he said with a smile that was arrogant, yet forgiving. Who was the grown-up here? Who was corrupting who? I swallowed.

My eyes dropped to my keyboard, and I struggled for a steady breath. I was shit-scared and turned on. Apparently, this was the perfect combination to make me produce small moans resembling a cat in heat.

"Why me?" I asked.

Jaime remained motionless, but his stare nipped at the sensitive flesh of my neck, tickling my lower abdomen. "Because," he said slowly, his soft lips parting as he drank me in, "I want to fuck a teacher before I go off to college."

And just like that, ladies and gentlemen, my quivering thighs and glassy eyes suffered a bad case of ice-cold bucket of rage.

Standing up and folding my arms, I pinched my lips together to make sure a curse didn't escape them. "I'm sorry, James. I don't seem to register half of the things you've said today, because it sounds like you're begging to fail my class and get kicked out of school."

Now it was his turn to stand, and I shrank back toward the whiteboard when I remembered he had a good nine inches on me (also in his pants, if that prevailing rumor was right.)

"Sweetheart," he said, following that with a *tsk-tsk* of his tongue, his confidence unnerving. "Give me your worst. Fail me. Throw me in detention for the rest of the year. We both know it won't affect my graduation or my future. You'd only be shooting yourself in that lovely, sexy-as-fuck foot of yours."

His eyes moved to my legs, and he took a step forward. My throat constricted with an unfamiliar need to bite something. Preferably this HotHole's butt.

"The damage to the Range Rover is around eighty-five hundred dollars, thanks for asking," he continued, straight-faced.

Another step. *Thump, thump, thump*, went my heart. I was a flower and he was a rare sunray, and we were drawn to each other, reluctantly, unwittingly, disastrously. Every cell in my body sizzled, begging for his touch.

Jaime wanted to fuck a teacher, so what? I wanted to fuck a baller. We were two sensible grown-ups making a conscious decision...only he wasn't really a grown-up, was he? And I was anything but sensible to get into this mess.

But he had leverage on me.

And those piercing blue eyes.

Besides...I wanted him. He was the first thing that had made me feel giddy in a while. Since Julliard, to be exact.

How sad was that?

"Jaime," I croaked. "I'm sure there are other teachers you could...work your charm on. How about Ms. Perklin?"

She was about three centuries old and smelled like used dental floss, but I wanted to gauge his reaction, postponing what was beginning to feel inevitable. Jaime stopped when our toes touched, his dimpled smile broadening, the black eye barely visible. I might have an easier time rejecting him if he weren't a female lubricant, I thought while admiring his masculine jaw and high forehead.

"Correction..." His lips brushed mine as he leaned down, and

I shivered and stepped back, aware people might see us through the door's glass window. "I don't only want to fuck a teacher. I want to fuck my Lit teacher. She's got sass, great ass, long legs, and even though she thinks I haven't figured her out, I know that behind the prissy disguise is a woman who curses like a sailor and can out-drink anyone on my football team."

Damn right, I could. They were only teenagers. I had impressive binge-drinking mileage. Eras of destructiveness caused by dark times of depression. *But I digress.*

"Do you want us both to get kicked out of All Saints?" I inhaled, patting my sweaty palms on my navy polka-dot dress. Someone had to talk sense into this boy. Too bad it was *me* we depended on. My willpower was nonexistent in those days. I had very little to lose at this point, if at all.

He grabbed me by the waist and spun us around so his back shielded my whole body from the windowed door. He pulled me into him, and my body melted against his like hot butter.

"I won't tell," he whispered into my neck, making me shiver with pleasure. "Neither will you. A nice short fling, Ms. G. I'll move to Texas to play college football. You'll move on to an ugly-ass accountant with a good heart or some shit. Someone to make babies with. That's all. Now what do you say, Melody?"

I was about to say *dream on* but didn't have the chance.

Jaime dove down, his sultry lips breathing into mine. "On second thought, don't say a word. I'll see for myself."

Jaime Followhill kissed me, the most intoxicating kiss I'd ever had. The minute his mouth slammed over mine, my toes curled inside my sensible pumps. It wasn't just the urgency of his hot mouth or the sweet taste of his gum but also his drugging male scent. He invaded every inch of my pores, kissing me like he had something to prove, a point to make. I grabbed his smooth-cheeked face with abandon and inhaled, while he opened my mouth with his tongue and devoured me like I was his fucking last meal.

His tongue attacked mine, owning my mouth, licking every part and swallowing my needy moans. I wasn't surprised when his hand dug into my ass and he yanked me into his erection. He rubbed himself against me, shamelessly jerking off on me, grabbing one of my hands and placing it against his impressive cock.

It was wrong.

It was wrong, and I'd be lying if I said I didn't like how wrong it felt.

Whether I was corrupting or being corrupted…I loved how it made me feel.

My heart drummed with excitement and fear. I knew part of the thrill was the possibility we'd get caught. It felt like swallowing an eight ball of speed and washing it down with a dozen shots of vodka.

Hot fucking damn. Jaime Followhill had some moves.

"Anyone can see us," I muttered into another dirty-hot kiss. The space between us was already charged with sex, reeking of juices we barely kept hidden behind thin clothing. I was soaked and ready, and he'd released those male hormones that make teenage guys' rooms smell like jizz and sweat. Only on him, the smell was pretty magical.

"You're covered by me," he murmured into my neck, nipping my skin with his teeth and moving south. His tongue sliced through the valley of my swollen breasts like an arrow.

"Not true." My face was now on display for anyone to see.

"Meet you at your place in an hour."

"You don't know where I live." I hungrily skimmed my hands over his iron chest.

Jaime pulled away and gave me one of his mischievous grins.

Jesus. He was a stalker, too? I had to admit, I found it hot as hell. One of the sexiest guys at school…stalked me. Why did I have to be a teacher? Shit like that never happened when I was a student.

"No." My voice was resolute. With every second his lips weren't on mine, the fog of a building orgasm faded, making way for logic.

Hello, logic. You killjoy, you.

"Ms. Greene…" His forehead and nose were crushed against mine. We both panted, eye to eye, chest to chest. "You're about eight minutes too late to walk out of this arrangement. This…" His hand ducked under my dress hem and up between my thighs, and a finger traveled along my wet slit through my plain cotton under-wear (no lace today), stroking not pushing, in a torturous tease. "Is mine until school ends. I will eat it, fuck it, play with it, and sleep in it if I want to. And I want to. I wanna do all those things to you."

What horrified me the most about Jaime's statement was that I knew he was going to get his way. I had agreed to it before I'd even walked into detention today. He had too much power over me, and not only because of his social status. I'd always been aware of his beauty and powerful presence, but up until now, I used them to re-sent him. Now that they were offered to me, all bets were off.

"We're going to be exclusive. If I catch you spreading those toned legs for anyone else, he's gonna regret he was born with a dick."

Oh yeah? Was he going to resist all the temptation that was swarming around him like bad BO at Coachella?

As if reading my mind, he added, "My cock will only have two homes. Your mouth and your pussy. Ass, too, if you're feeling adventurous."

Mother of God.

"Detention's over. Take your stuff and leave," I gritted, taking one step back and then another.

He followed me and dipped his head, biting my neck before straightening and snapping his fingers. "Get in your car and drive home. I'll join you soon." He smacked my ass, turned around, and left, leaving a whiff of his singularly masculine scent.

I stood there, mouth agape, his taste still on my lips, the tingling of his touch still between my thighs as I rolled one thought around in my head: *Oh, Melody, you are so fucked.*

Luckily for me, I was about to get fucked even harder.

Chapter Three

I DIDN'T GO HOME.

Going home would be admitting defeat. I might technically have let Jaime take the blame for the car, but I hadn't initiated anything sexual with him. That was all on him.

What made my decision even easier was bumping into his mother on my way out.

I was headed to the parking lot when I spotted Principal Followhill watching me through her office window. I stabbed the entry remote, hysteria controlling my movements as I considered making a dash for my car when her icy voice seeped from the open window.

"Ms. Greene. A word?"

There was a soundless moment when I saw my life flash in front of me, and sadly, it was a short, shitty movie consisting of me sprawled out on my old couch watching *American Ninja Warrior*, showing up to family events dateless, and attending a weekly support group for former athletes (most of us were in various stages of drunkenness).

Ya know, fun times.

If Principal Followhill knew what had happened in detention, she was going to remove every internal organ in my body, restuff it with dynamite, and blow up the whole school. That's how much she hated me.

"Sure." I smiled big, throwing my arms in a *why-not* gesture and walking back toward All Saints.

Why not? Because she wants to kill you and because you just made out with her teenage son.

The minute I entered her office, I knew she was onto something. Her usually smooth Botoxed forehead looked like it had collapsed into a heap of extra skin.

"Sit."

I did.

"Ms. Greene, do you know why you're here?"

I was so nervous I couldn't breathe but somehow managed to shake my head no. Her office alone scared the shit out of me. It was so big, yet suffocating, with its heavy furniture of cherry-stained wood and burgundy leather and its ox-blood walls, everything a deep red, like Carrie had paid a visit there on prom night and lost.

Principal Followhill stood near a painting that probably cost more than my rent, her arms behind her back, and closed her eyes, exhaling. "The incident with my son, James."

Oh no. Please, no. I wasn't ready to die. I had so many things to see and experience. Most of them between the sheets with her barely-legal son, but still.

Jokes aside—I was pretty sure I peed myself a little. I was terrified. Not of getting fired, but of the consequences of pissing off someone with Principal Followhill's clout. My parents taught in the school district adjacent to Todos Santos. This was their home, and they were a vital part of this small, judgmental community.

I was about to screw my family because of a brief kiss.

"Principal Followhill, I can explain," I rushed to say, jumping up from my seat.

She launched in my direction and shoved me back into the chair. If I wasn't so consumed with guilt, I would've been floored that she touched me.

She held up her hand, her face pale. "No, you listen to me. James is a brat. Don't you think I know that? What he did to your car… he should have left a note after he hit you, not driven away. It looks bad, but he simply panicked. He explained it all to me. No need to file a police report. I assure you he's very, very sorry, and he's going back to the student-parking lot from now on. I'll write you a check for your repairs, and I'll, of course, compensate you for the inconvenience as well. I'll be damned if I'll allow one reckless decision to tarnish my son's reputation." She reached for her Hermès bag and plucked out a checkbook.

My eyes followed her movements like she was performing some trick of dark magic. Of course, I was a problem. She wanted it fixed, so she threw money at it. *At me.*

She didn't know about the kiss. All she knew was that Jaime came back home yesterday with a banged-up Range Rover and his own version of what happened in the parking lot. He'd kept his side of our deal.

"This little car mishap is not to leave these walls. Do you understand, Ms. Greene?" Principal Followhill bent down and scribbled on the check, her mouth twitching in annoyance. "You have a mouth, in case you didn't notice. You could use it and say something."

Why do you hate me? I wanted to scream. *What have I done to you?* Though I already knew the answer. She hated me because I wasn't royalty. I wasn't someone who was born and bred in Todos Santos. I was an outsider, contaminated and mortal, with middle-class parents. On top of that, I was a weak link who—because of my above-mentioned disadvantages—couldn't control my classes.

"Understood," I sniffed.

24

She fingered the check she'd written for me. Despite my best intentions, I plucked it from between her French-manicured nails and peeked. Ten K. Way, way more than necessary. *Bribe.*

We were all corrupted now. It made me a little less remorseful about making out with her son.

Jaime was blackmailing me.

And I was blackmailing his mother.

My parents always said money made people twisted and immoral. I used to think they were exaggerating. I was starting to believe that they weren't.

I stood up, smoothing my dress and jutting out my chin. Principal Followhill held my gaze but tugged at her ear. *Nervous. Desperate. Clueless.*

"All is forgotten?" Her lips barely moved.

"All is forgotten." I nodded, walking out of her office $10,000 richer.

I drove straight to a local bar.

After all, I had some money to burn. *And dirty little secrets to forget.*

Chapter Four

I WOBBLED BACK TO MY apartment building at midnight, my breath stinking of Bud Light and stale peanuts. Trying to fish for my keys, I halted in front of my door in the darkened hall-way, rummaging through my loaded handbag. When I finally felt the sharp edge of the key, I jerked out my Pointe shoe keychain and it clunked to the floor. Blowing a lock of my hair from my face in frustration, I sighed. It was going to be a bitch to retrieve. I was getting too old to get tanked.

But I didn't even have to bend down.

Because someone else picked my keys up for me. From behind.

My heart throbbed faster, yet I stilled, feeling the warmth of another body pressing against mine. The air pulsated with the vital-ity of an impending fantasy that was about to be fulfilled.

Fear and lust filled my veins with adrenaline and dopamine. The overlapping feelings made me heady, excited and aroused.

Crap. I couldn't resist him in my current state. His erection dug into my ass, and I swallowed.

I watched his hand unlocking my door from behind. His warm lips whispered into my ear. "Get in and get naked." It was an order.

The door flung open with a little push from his hand. I wanted to cry in excitement. Correction: I did actually cry in excitement. There were tears of joy in my eyes. What can I say? Booze and eighteen-year-old jocks who are hung like a horse made this girl hella happy.

I practically skipped into my living room/kitchen, which was decorated with brown boxes and my old couch. I had to move to hell-knows-where next month and was already starting to pack. Seeing my life crumbling, stuffed into half-filled cardboard containers, only made my decision to have sex with my student easier. It wasn't like I was ruining anything substantial I'd built. I was a loser, practically homeless and soon-to-be unemployed. An outcast. Jaime took the edge off of the reality of my future.

I felt his huge form pacing behind me, ready to pounce at any moment.

I pulled off my polka-dot dress and threw it on the floor. Turning around, I looked at him for the first time, smiling under my lashes. Jaime did not return the playful smile. In fact, his brows were knit tightly together and his jaw so clenched, it looked like it was about to snap. He had a cut lip and dried blood coating his nostrils.

He fought. Again. Probably with Vicious, judging from the nasty welts and purple bruises.

"What happened to you?" I swallowed.

He ignored my question. "This is how you repay me for fixing up your shit, Ms. Greene?" His voice was dark and serious. Not at all like an eighteen-year-old's student.

"Jaime." My tone danced unevenly. Jaime…what? I stood him up. Even though I never did agree to meet him at my place. How long had he been waiting, anyway?

I was standing in my bra and underwear in my living room, dealing with a cranky teenager and was pretty fucking sauced. Another low I didn't think I was going to stoop to. I hugged my own waist, covering some of my skin.

"I like your bra," he said hoarsely, but it did not sound like a compliment. *It sounded like a threat.*

I looked down to examine the pink lace.

"It's my favorite. Victoria's Secret." I licked my lips, sounding dumber than an Adam Sandler character. I was so out of my element. Jesus. What the fuck was wrong with me?

"Come here," he demanded, pointing at the floor.

I paced in his direction, my eyes bugging out at the thrill. He was wearing dark Diesel jeans and a black muscle shirt with his gym's name on it. And flip-flops. I loved men who could pull off flip-flops. His bun was spectacularly messy, too.

When I got to him, I looked down. No toe hair. A keeper.

"Down on your knees, Greene." His voice still had a menacing edge to it.

Where did that come from? He was usually a pretty playful guy. In an I'll-fuck-you-over kind of way. I did as I was told, because… well, because at this point, I was pretty much the Followhills' bitch. *Sit, bend, cash checks, forget secrets, kneel down.* I was lucky they hadn't asked me to scoop dog poop from their front lawn.

"I have a blow job with your name on it for making me wait here like a soft dick." He brushed a brown curl from my face.

"I don't do blow jobs. I have a really bad gag reflex," I answered truthfully. Seriously, I'd found out about it the hard way during high school. Never had a corn dog or a banana since.

Calm and collected, he unzipped and lowered his jeans, releasing his hard, swollen cock out of his Calvin Klein black briefs.

Holy shit, it was beautiful. Not nine inches like the cheerleaders were whispering about in class (they sucked at geometry, that should've been my first clue) but almost—it was just picture-perfect. Postcards-and-stamps worthy. He had the sleekest, smoothest shaft, a prominent head, and a thick velvety vein. And a tilt. To the right.

Perfect, perfect, perfect.

And he fucking knew it, the bastard. That was why he displayed his dick to me like it was the *Mona Lisa*.

I took a brief moment to process the fact that I had my student's one-eyed snake staring right back at me in the middle of my tiny empty apartment. Worst part? *Still giddy and excited.*

My throat bobbed.

"Maybe I can make an exception, since you took a bullet for me and all." I rolled my eyes, feigning amusement. But there was nothing amusing about that cock. It was serious. Things were about to go down, literally and figuratively.

The only problem was…I didn't know how to give head. I think Jaime figured it out himself, because he tugged at my hair toward his groin.

"Start licking," he instructed.

I did. His flesh was hot and silky under my keen tongue. I circled his cock's head hungrily with my eyes closed, feeling it jumping in delight to the movements of my mouth. After a minute, Jaime picked up my hand and curled my fingers around the base of his shaft. Would you look at that? My Lit student was giving me a sex-ed lesson.

"Pump," he groaned.

I did. I wondered how many of my female students had sucked him off. Probably a lot. I wished I could say I didn't care, but that would be a lie, so I tried to convince myself I cared because it made me feel inexperienced.

"Now suck, in and out," he whispered, grabbing the back of my head and moving it back and forth.

Every time I went in, his cock hit the back of my throat and I struggled for air…but I loved it. My underwear was once again damp with want. Logically, I knew this wasn't okay. But if it was so wrong…why did it feel so right?

Jaime kicked one of his flip-flops off and dug his toe into the fabric of my underwear. It was humiliating…and so fucking hot. He used his toe to lower the waistband of my undies with a loud growl. Once my sex was exposed, his toe honed in on my clit.

"Shit, fuck, Jaime." I did *not* sound like his teacher. Didn't feel like one, either. "What are you doing?"

"Making you come. Keep sucking, Greene."

I licked and sucked and got addicted to the sounds that left Jaime's mouth. I gave in and gave it my all. He kept on rubbing his toe against my swollen clit, and the feeling of an impending orgasm fired every nerve-ending in my body. My knees shook with pleasure, and I greedily rubbed my pussy against his toe. I was sure my OB/GYN would have a lot to say about the hygiene of this act, but at that moment, none of that mattered.

Not even the nagging suspicion that he might've done this so he could brag to his friends and humiliate me in front of the whole school.

"I'm going to come in your mouth, and you're going to come on my toe."

He was so filthy.

It was beautiful.

Just when the warm liquid shot into my throat, I felt a sharp pain as my bra was torn from my body from behind. I gasped in horror, swallowing his salty hot cum and opening my eyes at once, shocked.

He fucking tore my favorite bra. *On purpose.*

Jaime used his toe to nudge me to a reclining position on the floor, and I collapsed, rubbing the pink skin where he'd pulled off my bra.

"What the hell!" I screamed but was silenced by a kiss. A dazzling kiss that was followed by the two strong fingers he shoved into my pussy. I clenched around him, watching him move his head south and graze my hard nipples with his teeth.

"That's for keeping me waiting. I don't take well to tardiness."

The fucker was late to ninety percent of the classes I taught him!

"Well, I don't take well to assholeness," I muttered.

"I'll make it up to you. I'm a master at oral sex." Jaime's perfect skillful mouth said, his serene blues scanning me earnestly.

"How so?" I raised an eyebrow as he inched closer to my pussy, still pumping his fingers to the rhythm of my thudding heartbeat.

He gave a light shrug. "Spent summer camp last year eating pussy at Park City, Utah's most exclusive teen retreat. Campers, counselors, even a fucking park ranger. Twenty-six of 'em."

That was probably one of the most disgusting things I'd ever heard, but I was having too much fun to care.

"Not all women like the same things in bed," I croaked when his face was level with my pussy.

"True, but all women like *me* in bed." Jaime punctuated his cocky grin with a wink, reached for his jeans, pulled out something small, ripped it open—was it a condom?—and tossed it into his mouth.

"I know what you want, Ms. Greene. You want to come undone. I'll make you come. And with me, you'll never be done."

He dove in.

Jaime's cold, minty mouth met my hot-as-sin flesh. My hips bucked, chasing his touch as he sucked hard on my clit before breathing the fresh bite of mint into my pussy, driving his tongue deep inside. I tried to wriggle free, the intensity of my pleasure so profound I felt like I'd combust into burnt marshmallow under his body. But he pinned me down, placing a flexed muscular arm over my stomach, insisting I see this through with him.

It was tantalizing, the wave of weakness and lust that crashed over my body, head to toe. I gripped his long blond hair—so soft and shiny—in my small fist and jerked him closer into me, letting out a desperate mewl. A violent orgasm ripped through me, my muscles tightening in pleasure.

Jaime pinned me to the floor and crawled on top of me, devouring my mouth with his. "Taste it," he growled like a beast, disposing of his gum in my mouth. His tongue was everywhere—my teeth, the walls of my mouth, on my chin, even my cheeks. "It tastes like you, *Teach.*"

I chewed on his gum. He was right. It tasted like my pussy.

Thrill sliced through my veins when Jaime raised his body and fumbled for his jeans. I prayed he was actually searching for a condom this time. I wanted to fuck him more than I wanted to hit the lottery jackpot, but I was still too flushed, my nerves too sensitive after my mind-blowing orgasm.

He rolled on a condom and guided his cock between my folds until his balls hit my entrance.

"Missionary, huh? What kind of camp was it? 'Book of Mormon' Youth?" I egged him on.

He laughed, hissing a moan, his eyelids half-mast as he started thrusting, finding the tempo that made us both groan. He was the perfect size. Big and thick, but not scarily so.

"Baby, I'm just breaking you in for the future." He bit my earlobe, his damp chest sticking to mine. "Once I'm done, you'll be begging for missionary."

I believed him.

The sex lasted nearly fifteen minutes, a lot longer than I thought an eighteen-year-old, even one who'd just gotten off from a blow job, would be able to last. He came again, and after flipping him so I was on top, watching his gorgeous, Channing-Tatum-meets-Ryan-Gosling face as I clutched his cock, so did I.

When we were done, I rolled back and lay on the floor beside him. He had one hand tucked under his head and the other on his stomach. Everything about him was so perfect. Even his blond armpit hair was sexy. And that made me sad, because I knew guys like Jaime grew up to find women who were just as put-together as they were.

And these type of women? I wasn't among them.

He stared at my popcorn ceiling in contented silence.

"Say something." I cleared my throat, glaring. I had my head propped on one arm behind my head, my chest still dancing up and down. We were both naked, and it was starting to get chilly on my floor. But I wanted him to speak. Needed him to, badly.

"I've just fulfilled a fantasy." He slanted his head so we were looking at each other. "I think I'm allowed a moment to regroup."

"I was your fantasy?" How could that be? He was perfect, rich, and handsome. Young and sexily dangerous. And I was...*his boring teacher*.

"Ms. Greene..." he started, cupping my cheek.

I leaned into his hand before I realized what I was doing. By the time I felt his warmth against my skin, it was too late to pull away. "Please, call me Mel when we're alone."

His lips twitched, but he fought his smile. "Mel," he corrected. "You're it. You're so. Fucking. It. Smart, sassy, and witty, and un-impressed with all the wealth and bullshit drama around you. You have no idea how hot you are. Which makes you even hotter. This is fucking happening, baby. *We're* happening."

I nuzzled into his neck, knowing that I was fueling a delusion that was just waiting to explode into calamity but not giving a damn anymore. His words moved something inside me. Not gently, either. They shook me to the core.

"Just until school ends," I whispered into his warm muscular shoulder, trying to convince myself more than him. He brushed his thumb along my back, sending goosebumps to my arms and scalp.

"This ends the last day of school," he agreed.

We had a deadline.

We had a plan.

And for a moment there, our warm bodies on that cold floor, with the haze of sex and bliss clouding our minds, I believed we were going to keep our careless promise. There was a little earthquake—a literal one—that moved some of the boxes as we made this agreement. I thought it was a coincidence. It wasn't. It was the devil in hell down below, rattling the earth with his laughter. Laughing at *me*.

At how wrong I was.

Chapter Five

THE NEXT WEEK AT SCHOOL was paradise. My classes were perfectly behaved. I didn't struggle to hold the students' attention, because my new fuck-buddy, an intimidating senior jock who made people fall in line with his stare alone, spread the word not to mess with Ms. Greene. No one was ballsy enough to ask why. Everyone naturally assumed my fucked-up car and his freshly painted Range Rover and its retreat to the student parking lot were the answer to that question. To them, Jaime wanted to keep me happy since he bumped into my car.

No one suspected we were bumping a few other things in our free time.

I taught all my classes then sat with Jaime in detention. I used the time to work, while he used the time to text. On the last day, I kept glancing at my watch, tapping my Sharpie against my desk. I couldn't concentrate on anything with him in the room. There were no words spoken between us. When his time was up, we both picked up our belongings and walked out of the classroom. I went to my car, he went to his, but by the time I got home, he was waiting inside my building, his hands shoved into the pockets of his jeans.

"Would you like to come in?" I sloped my chin down, biting a smile. He, too, grinned at his shoes. We were giddy. I liked that. I liked that and I hated that I liked that.

"Nah…I can't. Football practice for the exhibition. The Kings are going to kill those pussies playing next year for the Saints if we don't pull their shit together. Trent's pissed. A scout's coming to watch the game and look at his leg. They might reconsider his scholarship now that his rehab's done. Seven okay?"

"Seven's perfect."

He nodded. We stood there, staring at one another, before he shrugged and closed the space between us with a long step. "Screw this shit, I missed those lips."

Then came a hard, desperate kiss where his lips assaulted mine for a good minute.

Breathlessly, I unlocked my door and disappeared behind it, pressing my back against it with a sigh.

That didn't feel forbidden, or bad. Just a boy and a girl liking each other.

He came back at ten after seven, and for every extra second I waited, anxiety and disappointment built in my gut. I opened the door, frowning. "You said seven. I hate tardiness."

"That makes two of us." He roughly pushed me into my apartment, oozing charged energy. "So, about that missionary position…" The quarterback giant stepped into my orbit.

His cut lip and new purple welt were even more prominent with the pink flush on his cheeks after a grueling workout, and his hair still wet from the shower. Between footfall and Defy, there were a lot of injuries among the HotHoles. A broken ankle had ended Trent Rexroth's football career in the fall. That happened in a locker-room accident. But it was almost like Jaime *wanted* to fuck up that pretty face of his. The Saints practiced and scrimmaged even in the winter, but he was a senior. He and his friends wouldn't be part of the team next year.

"Flip your dress up."

I did, without even blinking. *He* should've been the teacher with that kind of authority. Exposing my baby blue panties, I awaited further instructions.

"Turn around and bend down to touch your toes, Little Ballerina."

I had no fucking clue how he knew I was a dancer, and asking him about it would force me to deal with the truth.

That he was a crazy stalker.

And that I absolutely liked that about him.

So, I just did as I was told, my ass in the air, presumably level with his groin. The throbbing ache between my thighs demanded release. I felt his fingers clutching my pussy from behind. He ripped my underwear off in one go and served them to me from behind.

"Still wet, despite my tardiness." He rubbed them against my lips. "Not that mad, I see."

Shit. The wet spot was obvious, even now, when my panties were merely a string.

"Can you please stop tearing my stuff apart? Not everyone's under mommy and daddy's financial wing." Goodie. The cat was out of the bag now.

He laughed, his abs bouncing against my ass, then thrust three fingers at once into my entrance, making me stumble forward. He caught me by the shoulder before I fell headfirst.

"This week was an introduction," he warned. "Today...today, baby, I'm marking you as mine."

It sounded crazy. And hot. *Crazy hot*, actually. I was immediately game. If I was going to fuck up my career, better enjoy the ride, right?

"Let's see your ballerina's balance as I fuck every other guy you've ever had out of you."

With that, I heard his zipper rolling down as he freed his cock from his pants. His bulging head found the lips of my pussy, and I quivered in anticipation, lifting up slightly to gain more balance.

"Hands. On. Toes." He bit the crook of my neck from behind and drew circles with his tip around my pussy, making me mad with need. He was also fucking bare.

"Jaime, wrap up and get in before I die." My voice trembled.

"Shh," my stalker said, ripping the condom wrapper with his teeth, still teasing my entrance from behind. "You just keep holding on to those toes, ballerina. I'll take care of the rest."

He went in slow. Painfully slow. Every inch of him took a second to go in, then slid back even slower. My legs quivered. I cried out in pleasure and frustration. This was torture of the highest level, but I was enjoying every minute.

"Faster," I begged under my breath.

He wouldn't listen. The next time he went in, it was even slower.

"Jaime." I bit my lower lip. "Fuck me like you mean it."

"Then act like you fucking want it," he growled, grazing my shoulder with his teeth. "Don't stand me up. Don't give me shit when I'm ten minutes late, and don't try and act like you don't want this."

Inch. Another inch. Another inch. It was a beautiful torture. I wanted to push him away and run to my bedroom to finish my business with my plastic boyfriend, Victor the Vibrator. But I wasn't strong enough to resist him, no matter what he did to me.

"Fine," I grunted. "Fine, I promise. Now fuck me."

"That's better," he murmured, thrusting himself all the way in and making me stumble. He gathered my hair into a ponytail and jerked my head upward, pulling my body close to him so I wouldn't crash. Then he fucked me so hard I felt numb from the waist down before he was done with me.

That's what happens when you come seven times in one night, I thought as I wobbled toward my bed. By the time he went home, around midnight, I couldn't feel my clit. Or my legs. Hell, not even my feet.

But he'd made his point crystal clear. And me? I wanted him to make it all over again.

Chapter Six

DAYS FILLED WITH CHAIN ORGASMS and hurried kisses in hidden corners and deserted classes ticked by. A blur of bliss and danger, abandoned lust. The trick was not to think about it. Any part of it. Not about my future—as a teacher and an adult—or about what I was doing. And *definitely* not about who I was doing it with.

No longer in detention, Jaime found other creative ways to stick around after school and spend time with me. Mostly, we fell into a routine where he visited me at my apartment after his football drills with next year's team.

Three weeks into our affair, when another Saturday rolled around, I was glad he had other plans. I finally mustered enough fake bravado to collect my thoughts and try and make sense of it all. The Saints were playing an exhibition scrimmage against the Kings of Sacramento, and technically, I could've supported my local team and watched Jaime play but decided against it. Putting some space between us and reminding myself that this was just casual fun was in my best interest. His too.

Besides, I'd made my own plans to meet my parents at an Italian joint in downtown Todos Santos this evening.

I did pass by the game on my way to Target that afternoon, taking the long way just so I could catch a glimpse of the game. I tried to convince myself it wasn't about Jaime. Football was a big deal at All Saints High. But no matter how you looked at it, when I stopped at the red light and glanced across the road to the field, I was looking for number four. For Jaime Followhill. For the HotHole who always made my stomach dip like I'd just gotten on a rollercoaster. For the boy who felt too much like a man. And, sadly, for the guy who filled the void in me with more than just his arousal and hot flesh.

I found him standing on the sidelines, chewing on his mouthguard with his hands on his waist while nodding at something coach said to him. He looked distracted, and if I had the courage, I'd want to believe it was me he was thinking about.

His body looked cut and perfect, even through his jersey.

It was worrisome. I should have known right there. The way I smiled to myself, like I owned him in some way. Like this perfect creature, that was now yelling to his friends from the sideline, looking animated, looking *perfect,* was under my spell.

I kept on staring until someone behind me honked and I had to speed away, hitting the gas pedal too hard. Just then, Jaime twisted his head in my direction, as if he heard it too.

It was ridiculous. There was no way he could know I was watching him. The place was crowded as hell and the parents and students of All Saints High were very vocal about their local team.

But that didn't soothe the blush that crept up my neck and spread through my cheeks.

Nothing did. For the remainder of the day.

My parents and I had dinner, during which they asked about when my contract with the school would be renewed (*probably never?*), when I might find a man (*ditto, but hey, I found a hot boy who knows how to go down on a woman thirteen different ways*), and why my cheeks were so flushed (*see the answer to question number two*).

It wasn't bad, per se. The food was great. The company…well, made me feel like the biggest letdown humanity had to face.

That was the thing about being Celia and Stewart Greene's daughter. The minute my dream of becoming a ballerina died, so did their pride in me. I was never quite good at anything else, and I guess they knew that.

They made sure I remembered it, too.

It wasn't an excuse for why I was like this. Unmotivated and sarcastic, but it definitely didn't help.

The three of us walked back to our cars and passed by the central fountain in downtown Todos Santos across from Liberty Park, the home to a semi-famous lake and alarmingly aggressive swans. Teenagers were always roaming there on weekends, playing loud, shitty music. (Guess that was one reason why the swans were prone to attacking.) Not that night, though. That night, it was worryingly quiet.

My parents and I were about to round a corner and head to the parking lot when I saw Vicious's silver Mercedes-Benz McLaren slicing past us. I couldn't miss the 500K vehicle because HE WAS DRIVING ON THE FUCKING SIDEWALK opposite from us.

The kid was honking his horn at people like his daddy owned this town. Unfortunately, his daddy *did* own this town. Vicious's father was so rich he hit lists like *Forbes* and shit every single year.

Maybe that's why his son felt entitled to hit everything and everyone else, I thought bitterly.

Pedestrians made way and let him pass through, accepting his behavior with bent heads. Everybody knew who he was, and more importantly, who he was going to be—a powerful, lawless cretin and the heir to a huge portion of the business interests in Todos Santos.

My parents and I skidded to a halt, our mouths shaping into stunned *O*s. We stared as my student parked on the grass, got out of his car, and strode toward a row of kids on their knees near the lake.

Well, fuck me sideways scissor-style. The older jocks were standing above the teenagers on the ground, yelling animatedly and pushing each other, on the verge of breaking into a huge fight.

I saw Jaime there. My eyes were drawn to him immediately, on instinct, before my mind even processed what I was staring at. He was leaning against the gazebo, exchanging hushed words with Dean Cole and Trent Rexroth, the former captain of the football team, who had his leg in a fresh-looking cast. Shit. He'd broken it again? What happened at the game today?

Jaime, Trent, and Dean kept to themselves, furrowed brows and brooding expressions on their faces. I recognized some of the kids on their knees, their heads down in surrender and their arms behind their backs. All failed, aspiring, or younger football players at All Saints High.

The Four HotHoles were up to something, I knew. And it didn't look like this was a voluntary game, like Defy.

It looked serious.

Vicious unrolled the sleeve of his white tee and took his soft Camel pack out of it, lighting a cigarette and squatting down, blowing smoke into the face of one of the kids who sat on their knees, awaiting the verdict. The guy gasped and choked on a cough but didn't dare move an inch. It looked like an ISIS execution line, and I knew I had to do something. The police chief was a kiss-ass friend of Baron Spencer Senior, Vicious's father, so calling the cops would have gotten me nowhere. But I couldn't just stand there and watch this happen. Right?

Right?

Vicious walked slowly along the row of suspects, his arms

behind his back. "Listen up, fuckers. I know the Kings weren't the dickbags who greased the floor under Trent's locker. That's twice someone targeted him. The captain of your fucking team, you sorry-ass bitches."

He was so mad, he spat as he spoke. I watched the saliva flying out of his mouth, illuminated by the Victorian lamppost.

"Last time I figured this was an attack from a rival team to keep him from playing. Eliminate the competition." Vicious took another drag and spat near one of the meatheads on the end with a red varsity jacket and a baseball cap turned backwards. "But Trent's graduating. No reason for another team to take him out now."

Some of the teens were crying as they looked down to the dewy grass, and some were moaning in pain. They weren't bleeding, they didn't look beaten up. Well, not physically, anyway. But Jesus, this kid was as fucking intimidating as Satan himself.

"I. Will. Find the fucker who greased the floor!" he shouted.

The jocks on their feet behind him roared, pumping their fists in the air. Jaime, Dean, and Trent were still deep in conversation. Luckily, they weren't feeding the troll.

"I WILL punish the motherfucker," Vicious screamed maniacally, thumbing his chest and looking around for support.

"Fuck yeah!" The jocks raised their hands, slurring into the night.

"And by the time we're done with him, he will be sorry his whore of a mother ever gave birth to him!"

"Yes! Yes! Yes!"

I had chills up and down my arms. I hated Baron Spencer. According to Coach Rowland, he wasn't even a very good football player, and I doubted he cared about the team that much. No. This whole nightmare of a night was orchestrated because he was a sadistic, violent fuck.

My mother yanked my white blouse and gritted, "I know some

of these kids. They go to All Saints High. They are your students, Melody. You can't let this happen."

"The screaming one in the skinny jeans is Baron Spencer," I whispered back. "His daddy owns this town."

"Doesn't matter." My father shook his head, resting his hand on my shoulder. It felt so much heavier than it actually was, and I knew why. "This is about your integrity, Mel."

Oh, fuck. That old thing.

I knew I had to step in. I also knew I was about to be royally humiliated in front of my parents. Vicious feared me just a little less than he feared a Chihuahua in a pink tutu. Meaning, he wouldn't give a damn about me butting into this mess.

I crossed the road on shaky legs. Vicious's ruthless voice was still booming in my ears, getting louder with each step I took. My spine crackled, but I moved forward.

"Rat out the asshole who's responsible, or each and every one of you fuckers goes back home with a permanent mark." He pointed his cigarette at his potential victims. A few ballers behind them hauled them up to their feet by their hair, and the captives cried in agony.

Vicious stopped in front of a heavy guy, who had tried to make it onto the football team last year, and inched the burning ember of his cigarette toward the guy's forehead.

They are your students, Melody. You can't let this happen.

My dad was right.

"Baron!" I hurried, lightly jogging from the crosswalk into Liberty Park. He was not going to hurt the kid. Not on my shift.

Vicious didn't even have the courtesy to turn around and check to see who called him. "Take all suspects to the gazebo behind the parking lot for interrogation." His voice was clipped and low.

That gazebo was isolated, a deserted, scary place where no one set foot at night. Bastard had a touch. No surprises there.

"Baron Spencer!" I raised my voice, only a few feet away from him now. Some of the students cleared out of the way for me, but the majority just snickered as I raced toward the teenager from hell. They were more scared of him than they were of me. I couldn't blame them. "Stop this immediately! Let these boys go!"

When I reached him, he finally turned around, his face painted with boredom and pity.

When I didn't back down, his expression darkened. Vicious might not be as beautiful as Jaime, Trent, and Dean, but he somehow had the most memorable face. He looked like a guy whose shit list you didn't want to be on. I swallowed hard, hating myself for feeling intimidated by him.

"I'm sorry, remind me who the fuck you are?"

Of course he knew who I was. I taught him Lit every day, which is what made everyone around us laugh, pointing their beer bottles and Solo cups at me. Even his fucking captives chuckled.

I'm doing this for you, assholes.

Heat spread up my neck, and my hand tightened around my anchor necklace, as it did every time anger washed over me. I did everything in my power not to look at Jaime, because I was afraid to see what was written on his face. Was he laughing at me like all the rest?

"Do it now, or I'm calling the police," my voice barely shook.

Vicious took a step forward, his face so close to mine I saw the crazy dancing in his irises. His eyes, black like an abyss, threatened to pull me to the dark side. I dug my heels deeper into the grass and balled my hands into fists. My body hummed with adrenaline. This was happening. I was standing up to him.

"I fucking dare you, sweetheart. Go ahead, test me. Actually, I'd love for you to do that. It'll get you kicked out of your job, and I won't have to see your sour-ass face every day."

That was it. I was so pissed that I wasn't above punching his smug face. I stepped back, fishing out my cell phone from my bag. So what if they fired me? They weren't going to renew my contract anyway.

A warm, familiar hand stopped me before my fingers dialed 911. "Apologize," Jaime's voice commanded.

But the order wasn't aimed at me.

Vicious tipped his head back and snorted, his straight teeth on full display. "Tanked again, Followhill? Jesus. It's not even midnight yet."

"You better do it," Jaime sing-songed, ignoring the jab, stepping into his BFF's face. Nose to nose now, their gazes dripped defiance. "Unless you want out of the HotHoles."

I was baffled, to say the least. Two bullets in less than a month this guy had taken for me. Vicious and Jaime were locked in a staredown. Vicious glowered under his devilish brows, begging Jaime to let it go—every muscle in his face quivering in anger—but Jaime wouldn't back down. Finally, after a whole minute at least, it came. Sweet and orgasm-worthy.

"My bad, Greene." Vicious's words were sharp and insincere as his shoulder brushed past Jaime's. He looked like it physically pained him to say them.

As much as his indifferent act sprinkled fear-dust on everyone's heads at school, he was still mortal. Capable of feeling the loss of his best friend. And Vicious knew the truth. People didn't like him, not really. They loved Jaime, Dean and Trent. The handsome, funny, wholesome jocks he hung out with.

He needed them.

But something told me that they needed him, too.

"Apology accepted. Now, break this thing up immediately." I smoothed my blouse, arching one eyebrow and slanting my head to his captives.

"No," Jaime said firmly, turning around to face me.

I allowed myself to drown in his face, even if for only a second. We were back to acting like a teacher and a student, playing our roles, but I knew those lips which he now rolled inward, probably to suppress words he should never say to his educator. Knew how they tasted and what they were capable of doing under my thin, worn blanket.

"Sorry, Ms. Greene, but you'll have to sit this one out. This is a team matter. I give you my word, it won't rub off on you. Someone screwed Trent over." He shook his head, his lips pinching in annoyance. "We need answers."

"Mr. Followhill—"

"No," he said, cutting me off. "You lose." The last sentence came out soft, and what came after was even softer. "Next time I catch you stalking me from across the road," he whispered into my ear, close enough for it to look suspicious but not enough for people to talk about it afterwards, "you better come say hi. Better yet, you better show me how much you miss me with your lips, instead of stripping me with your eyes."

There wasn't anything I could do about Vicious and his dangerous tricks, and I knew it. The HotHoles always took care of their own. Trent was injured again, and someone had to pay. I had very little power over the students of All Saints, but I very much doubted anyone else, including Principal Followhill herself, would be able to stop them from seeking retaliation.

Slowly, without breaking eye contact with him, I backed down, until I finally turned around and walked back to my parents, who were still waiting on the other side of the road.

"Well?" My mother elbowed me, her eyes shimmering the same healthy curiosity she had about almost every subject matter in the world.

"I took care of it." I avoided her gaze, pretending to look for something in my bag. Maybe it was my dignity I was looking for.

Either way, Vicious had won.

And Jaime helped him.

But not at my expense. And that was something.

That was a lot.

Chapter Seven

I SPENT THE WEEKEND WONDERING what happened to the poor bastards the Four HotHoles had interrogated at Liberty Park and whether my face-off with Jaime and Vicious would change the pact between me and my fuck-buddy. My fingers tingled to text him and ask all those things, but I knew it was risky.

Was I angry at him? Was the incident a wake-up call, reminding me that we were so different? That he was still a teenager, taking tentative steps toward becoming a man? These were exactly the kind of questions I didn't want to deal with. No. I was biding my days, clinging to the weekend in the hope distance and time would wash away the fog of lust between us, making room for logic and rationality.

Monday was the best day of my entire career. Everything ran smoothly, and when I reached the last class with Jaime and his friends, they all behaved.

Everyone…other than Jaime.

He was messing with his phone, as usual. Since he wasn't looking at me, I let it slide. I wanted to teach this class without feeling my nipples puckering under his scorching gaze.

My phone on my desk flashed. I resisted the urge to check it, focusing on Millie, who was standing up, reading a poem she'd written. She was good. A creative spirit, with an artistic flare that poured through every cell in her body. Did she want to write? Maybe paint? Her textbooks and hands were always decorated with doodles, her nose always buried in a book. With the right guidance and nurturing, she could do great things.

I knew without a shadow of a doubt that I wasn't the person to bring them out of her. I lacked motivation, compassion, and authority, the three qualities that made a great teacher.

As I stared at her, I realized that even Vicious was quiet when she spoke. She had the kind of quirky charm a girl couldn't fake. Everyone's eyes were on her, which allowed me to sneak a peek at my phone. In the words of Julia Roberts in *Pretty Woman*: Big mistake. Big. Huge.

Jaime:
I missed you this weekend. Thought your ungrateful ass would text me a thank you for saving you from the wrath of Vicious. Alas, I was wrong.

Wow. Did he have any idea how much trouble he could get us into if someone saw this text? Students and teachers had each other's numbers for professional purposes only. I ignored him and continued nodding at Millie, smiling tightly. *Ping,* another text came.

Jaime:
It's cute how you pretend to listen to Millie when I know your just waiting for the clock to hit 3 so I can bend you over that desk and fuck you so hard the windows will rattle.

Of course, I didn't grace that message with an actual answer.

Although, I was itching to correct "your" with "you're." The Lit teacher in me hated when people misspelled shit. Apparently, even during sexting.

My cheeks darkened, and I played with my anchor necklace, brushing it against my lower lip. I coughed, clearing my throat, and said, "Louder, Millie."

She looked around, anxious as I was, and reluctantly raised her voice with the next line. Her poem was pretty fascinating, actually. About life and death and the way the cherry blossom tree symbolizes both. Everybody was quiet and alert. Dean Cole had his elbows on his desk, leaning forward, drinking her words like they were oxygen. And Vicious? He looked at her like she was his.

But there was no point. The only thing my ears were tuned into was what I secretly hoped to hear—the sound of my phone vibrating against the table as another message came through.

Jaime:
Your nipples are so tight I could cut fucking diamonds with them, baby. It's a turn on when everyone can see what I do to you. In half an hour, I'm going to shove my hand into your pencil skirt and my fingers into that pussy. Digging into Ms. G's G-spot and hitting it again and again until you pass out from your orgasms.

I circled the table and leaned back against it facing the class, hoping they couldn't see the blush that was a daily challenge since the start of our affair. Jesus! *Affair?* That was a bit much. It wasn't an affair. I was fucking my student, and my future, all at the same time. Nonetheless, I couldn't stop. I scanned the classroom full of students, and his face was the only one that stood out in the sea of bland teenagers. I barely registered the other faces, lost in the fog of lust.

Another vibration. This time I waited a few seconds before I glanced his way and found him smirking at his phone. Asshole.

Jaime:
Then I'll take my hand out, let you lick my fingers one by one, suck on them hard, and beg for me to take you. But I won't. You'll have to go down on me first, and I'll make you choke on my cock until you can't breathe. How would you like that, Mel?

I was sweating. Sucking in short breaths. Millie finished reading her poem. She was still standing, expecting my feedback. All eyes were on me. She'd done a wonderful job from what I could decipher in my lust-induced haze, but the words wouldn't leave my mouth. I was truly afraid that I'd blurt out something about Jaime and his dick. It really was too fucking beautiful not to be celebrated by our fine nation.

"Millie," I started, clearing my throat when I realized my voice cracked. I heard Jaime softly chuckle in the back of the room. I was going to kill him when the class was dismissed. Her big, blue Bambi eyes followed my every movement as I spoke. "I thought it was brilliant. Your poem had a rhythm like heartbeats. It was…enchanting," I managed, my smile almost apologetic.

It wasn't the right thing to say. I needed to open this up for discussion, but I was having a hard time stringing together a coherent sentence while my panties were this wet. Damn Jaime and his texts.

Straightening my spine, I clapped my hands one time. "Let's hear your thoughts about Miss LeBlanc's poem. Anyone?"

Bzzz. Another vibration erupted. A handful of people raised their hands, and I chose Shelly, the girl who I knew wouldn't shut up, and therefore allowed me time to read my incoming text.

Jaime:

So lost. So confused. So fucking mine. Owning someone has never felt this good.

His words hit me hard.

Was I really his? It didn't feel like it. Like it was real. Maybe for him, it was. But for me? I was too scared of the consequences of truly having him to even consider it an option.

Lost. Confused. I felt all those things. Not just in that moment, but in general. Where was I going after this? I was a terrible teacher, and my students deserved better. What more, I cared enough about them to acknowledge the fact that I need to make room for someone more passionate. More caring. Someone who would take the Millies of the world and turn them into artists, and not keep them here, in the gray classroom, reading poems they could barely understand.

After Shelly babbled something for the sake of talking, and another student asked Millie a couple of questions, Vicious, who had his long legs crossed over the table, his boots nearly touching someone's back, held up his hand. My breath hitched. I didn't want him to shatter Millie's confidence. Actually, I wanted to talk to her about enrolling in a creative writing class I knew across town. I liked to believe I saw some of me in Emilia. She was delicate, artistic, and unfazed by the privileged environment she wasn't a part of. I had a weird urge to protect her from Vicious, but no one else was lifting their hands.

I wanted to strangle the sulky bully as I ground out a weak permission for him to speak. "Yes, Baron?"

Vicious's hooded eyes were on Millie as he played with one of his rusty metal rings—a part of his iconic serial-killer attire. He bared his teeth, expecting her to shrink back into her chair like the rest of them, but Millie was still standing, eyeballing him like he was a punching bag she was about to swing her fist into.

I fucking like this girl.

"I thought it was spectacularly awful," he said, tugging at his full lower lip.

She raised one lonely eyebrow, a smile on her pretty, round face.

"That's enough from you, Baron," I started, but Millie raised her hand.

"Please, Ms. Greene. Let him finish. What was so 'spectacularly awful' about my poem?" she asked him, and she sounded genuinely interested.

I cringed. Why was she doing this to herself?

Vicious slumped back in his chair, examining his rings. "Too wordy. Too many analogies. Some of them were corny. Ones we've heard a thousand times before. You've got talent, I'll give you that. Still." He shrugged. "Your writing's sloppy. Stick to painting."

"And what would you know about writing?" I snapped. It was my turn to ask. It wasn't like me to lose my temper during class, but Vicious was literally being vicious. The fact that he'd won on Saturday night at the park didn't help, either.

I think Jaime knew better than to continue sexting me, because he tucked his phone into his jeans pocket and frowned at Vicious, his expression screaming, *Shut the fuck up, man.*

"I know quite a fucking bit, actually," Vicious chirped, his face lighting up. Usually, his voice was like a straight line on a heart monitor, uncaring and flat. "Ass-kissing's never helped an author or a poet grow and develop. Constructive criticism does. Maybe you're in the wrong profession, Greene."

Fuck this shit. I was going to throw him into detention until he was seventy. I didn't even care that Jaime had just invited me to another sex-fest after school, and that all I could think about was his angry, swollen cock. I didn't want Vicious talking to me like this and more importantly—to Millie. The girl didn't deserve it.

"Pack your stuff, Baron. You're coming with me to see Principal Followhill after class. I hope you don't have any plans for the upcoming month, because you're going to spend it with your mediocre educator. In detention. Where you can explain to me all about good poetry and bad life choices. Like talking back to your teacher." I let loose a sugary smile and cracked open my notebook with the name list, looking for the next poor soul that had to share a poem with class.

Trent groaned from his place on the other side of Vicious. "Good going, cunt. You just had to talk shit, didn't you? We've got team business to handle. Did you forget?"

"Language, Rexroth. Or you're up next."

I got ballsy. I had a back. It was Jaime. Who, by the way, looked just about ready to explode, staring down Vicious like he had just slaughtered a basket full of kittens. There was fire in his eyes, and it scorched everything it landed on. The bell rang, filling the class with laughter and noise, and people shoved their stuff into their backpacks.

"Mr. Linden, you'll be reading your poem next time. Class, I want you to read *The Rules of Poetry* by Michaela Steinberg and know it by heart for next class. There'll be a quiz," I barked into the chaos of teenage chatter.

Students poured into the hallway, but Jaime stayed put in his chair. His clenched jaw suggested someone in the room was about to get killed. Vicious was the only one still there other than us, and he took his time, stuffing his bag deliberately slow with a grin so big you'd think I was about to escort him to an exotic vacation on an island populated by strippers and international arms dealers.

I dropped Vicious at Principal Followhill's office and got back to class. I think she was both impressed and horrified with me call-ing Vicious on his bullshit. I had no idea how she was going to deal with him, but I didn't care, either. I'd done my part.

The minute I walked back into my classroom, I heaved a sigh. "What did you do to those kids the other night?"

Jaime sprawled back in his chair. He was wearing navy Dickies, high-top sneakers, and a purple muscle shirt that showed off his corny tattoo of a stupid-ass quote he had inked on his ribs. I'd never bothered reading it, but wouldn't be surprised if it was something from *SpongeBob Squarepants*.

Who cares? He was my own personal calorie-free dessert.

At least, that's what I tried to reduce him to in my mind.

Most of the time it worked.

But the more we spent time together, the more I needed to feed myself this lie.

"Come here." He crooked his index finger at me.

"Excuse me? I'm the teacher," I teased, happy to have him alone.

"And I'm the pissed-off guy who needs to put you in your place every now and again. Here." He patted his desktop and plopped back in this chair. I glanced at the closed door and back at him.

"Vicious could come back," I argued.

"Vicious would keep his mouth shut even if he walked in on me fucking Mr. Pattinson while the PTA president licks my asshole. I can do anything with anyone as long as it's not Millie. We're goddamned near blood-brothers."

Millie, huh? Maybe the bastard did have a beating heart after all.

I took slow steps to him and sat at the edge of his desk. He grabbed me by the waist and pulled me into his groin so that I straddled him, my legs curling around his waist.

"What did you do to them?" I whispered again, my hands buried in his golden hair as my arms circled his neck. Despite everything, I cared about those kids.

"Baby…" He brushed his knuckles against my lips, his eyes focused solely on them.

"Well?" I deliberately widened my eyes, questioning him.

He laughed like he thought my expression was cute. "Nothing yet. But we got a name. Toby Rowland."

"And?" Rowland was a junior, another douche who I taught. He was also Coach Rowland's son.

Jaime shrugged. "Dude's always hiding behind his daddy in practice. It'll be hard to pin him down, but neither one's getting away with what they did to Trent. Fuckers killed his ticket out."

Trent Rexroth, All Saints' stand-out football star, had slipped in the locker room before a big game this fall, breaking his ankle and ending his path to college and pro-football glory.

I opened my mouth, intending to convince him to give up the retaliation, but he grabbed me by my ass and pulled me into his aching erection, sucking hard on one of my breasts through the fabric of my blouse and finishing on a teasing bite.

"Shit…" I muttered.

"How was your weekend?" He placed his lips on my neck and licked his way to my cleavage. I shivered into his body. "Did you miss me?"

"It was good." My hands ghosted over his broad chest greedily. "And no," I lied. "I thought we agreed this was just harmless fun."

"It is." He tipped his head back, staring at me seriously. "And it's fun being with you."

"I bet it's just as fun being with high school girls." My mouth went dry when I said it.

It was stupid and insecure, but it felt good to finally say what I'd been thinking about for weeks. Where Jaime went, girls followed. Bronze-skinned, shiny-haired cheerleaders with wide smiles and legs for miles. They caught up with his long steps in the hallways, leaned against his SUV after school, and laughed at everything he said…even when he didn't make jokes.

Jaime smirked, his right hand tracing my inner thigh, traveling upward and disappearing under my pencil skirt. "I beg to differ. High school girls are high maintenance. They're full of drama. They talk about fucking hair straighteners and parties for hours. The hot ones make you go to Jennifer Love Hewitt movies. No. There's nothing fun about high school girls. You, on the other hand…"

His fingers found my soaking undies, and as usual, he cocked his head, smirking, letting me know that he was onto me. My body sang a tune only Jaime knew the words to and my heart drummed so fast and loud that I felt the pulse in my toes. Doing this was almost like begging to get caught.

A part of me was desperate to be seen.

"You talk back," he said. "You're cold and stubborn. Sad and snarky. I like your brand of weird. The whole package." He drew an imaginary circle with his finger around my face, leaning into me. "But most of all…" he breathed, placing a gentle kiss on the corner of my lips. "I like the chase. You make me sweat somewhere besides a football field. Turns out…that's the exercise I've been looking for."

Just as he said that, the door flung open and Vicious pushed his way inside. Lucky for me, he was staring down at a piece of paper he held in one hand and the ripped-open envelope he had in the other. "Can't believe she says shit like this," he muttered.

That allowed me a minute to jump off Jaime's boner and rearrange my skirt, leaning back down and pretending to flip through one of the books he had on his table. "Here's the paragraph you were looking for." I cleared my throat and straightened.

Vicious finally looked up, but it wasn't at me. "Trent just texted me. Coach called a team meeting. Toby's been named as captain for next year."

"Whatever." Jaime's jaw ticked. The atmosphere in the room changed. No words were spoken, but plans were being made, right in front of my eyes.

Toby Rowland was in so much trouble, it physically hurt me to think what they'd do to him once they got him alone.

"Whatever sounds right," Vicious echoed, his voice flat. "Thanks a fucking ton for detention, Ms. G. Hope you know what *you're* doing." He shook his head with a sadistic smile. *A threat.*

"Vicious," Jaime gnashed. *A warning.*

Vicious strode to his chair and flopped down, waving his hand. "She's lucky you have a soft spot for her. Otherwise I'd have reduced her to ashes at Liberty Park."

A hard spot, baby, I thought as I made my way back to my desk. *And you have no idea.*

Chapter Eight

THAT DAY CHANGED EVERYTHING, BECAUSE that day Jaime and I started texting. It made it so much easier to plan things. More hot dates at my partially-packed apartment. More fucking in insane positions. More stealing kisses at school, getting off on the thrill of being caught.

At the end of the week, Jaime sent me a picture of himself flexing his guns in front of the mirror in their locker room. I almost didn't open the text message, fearing I'd see something horrific like someone else's junk, but then I remembered it was Jaime I was talking about. He was oddly responsible for someone his age and with his status. Out of the four of them, he was the quietest. The one with the working moral compass. If Vicious was the evil one, and Dean was the stoner one, and Trent was the lost, beautiful soul searching for its mate, Jaime was the cement that glued them together. He was the guy you could always count on. And I was starting to count on him too.

Jaime:
It's scientifically proven. You're riding the best stud in town. These guns could kill.

Me:
Jaime, you're an eighteen-year-old. Perspective, please.

Jaime:
This from someone who goes to sleep with my dick clutched in her hand. Pizza tonight?

Me:
That happened once. By accident.

Me:
And yes. But no onions.

I leaned back against a box filled with books and giggled, hugging my cell phone like an idiot. *A disaster,* I thought to myself. *What the fuck are you doing? Dating him now?*

Jaime:
No onion? No condom then. I'm clean. Your on the pill.

Me:
YOU'RE. YOU-apostrophe-RE.

Me:
And deal.

Jaime:
Nice doing business with you. x

Dear God, I needed to stop this. Stop this before I was going to get hurt. Already, the way my heart squeezed every time I noticed him for the first time in class felt a little too hard. The pleasure of sleeping with him freckled with a dash of pain. He still filled me. Filled me with joy and laughter and amazing sex. But now he was sucking from me, too.

Emotions, thoughts, logic.

That evening, Jaime got to my apartment and tackled me to the sofa, peppering my whole face with kisses. I laughed, throwing my fists at his sculpted abs. We rolled around, half making out, half fighting and laughing, before we both stopped to take a breath, examining each other's faces for the first time since he walked in. He was atop of me, his eyes roaming my face, searching for answers to questions we were both too scared to ask aloud.

"How did you know I'm on the pill?" The silence rang so loud, I felt the urge to break it.

"Saw them on your bathroom counter. Duh."

"Well, let's get nekkid and do some dirty stuff then. I know it's Friday, and you probably want to hang out with your friends later." I grabbed the hem of my shirt and started getting undressed.

He stopped me, his palm on my hand. "Take it easy, missy. No rush. Let's watch a crappy nineties movie together while we wait for the pizza. I'm going to sleep here tonight."

I frowned. Vicious threw balls-out parties every weekend, and the HotHoles were always in full attendance. It was mandatory or some shit. I happened to know this because at All Saints getting invited to these things meant that you were one of the cool kids. I also happened to know there was a party tonight because yesterday the hallways were filled with hushed convos about which guys were going to be challenged to a fight in Defy and which girls were going to get inside Vicious's private media room where the HotHoles hung out.

"What about Vicious's party?" I asked. The last few weeks, the mere idea of having Jaime sitting there in the secluded room with young, willing women offering themselves to him made me lose my mind. I hated those parties, and despised Vicious even more for throwing them.

"I'm planning an even bigger party between your legs tonight." He wiggled his brows at me.

I rolled my eyes but couldn't help but smile. "I think I like you," I muttered, pressing my face to his muscled torso in a hug. I felt his heartbeat under my ear.

"I think I like you back."

My heart nearly exploded, and I found myself clutching the anchor on my necklace for dear life, knowing that this time, it couldn't save me from falling deeper into whatever the hell that was we were creating.

Actually, I knew exactly what it was.

Magic.

It's been psychologically proven. People lie to themselves in order to protect themselves from the things they do. From what they think and feel. I was in denial when it came to Jaime Followhill. In my head, I downplayed the whole thing. Reduced it to nothing but some fun. But the truth was, I was never so intrigued by a man.

Defy.

That's what I wondered about most. Why did he fight? He didn't look like the type who needed a violent outlet to unwind. Vicious, sure. But Jaime? No. He seemed like a laid-back guy.

So after the movie and pizza (no onions. He remembered), I asked him.

I prepped him beforehand. Knew that Jaime was not going to open up about things that had to do with his friends so easily. I got down on my knees and took him—all of him—deep in my mouth, covering most of his shaft, my fist doing the rest. He groaned and yanked my head back and forth, my hair in his fist.

"I'm going to come in your mouth," he announced. He stood, one foot lazily propped back against my fridge, in all his naked six foot three inch glory.

I moaned into his hot flesh, lolling my head from side to side. I liked it. To feel admired and desired by a younger man. He was driving me crazy…but I was driving him wild.

My moan encouraged him, and he emptied himself inside my mouth. The warm, salty liquid shot straight into my throat, and I swallowed it instantly, desperate for every drop of him.

After his release, he glided down the front of my fridge, sinking into a sit-down position, his knees bent, as he slowly let go of my hair. We both grinned, the kind of private smile only we knew how to decode. I doubted I could give that smile to someone else, even if I'd tried.

"What's up?" He grabbed my hand, offhand and confident, and jerked me to sit between his legs. I did, purring into his mouth as we shared a slow, seductive kiss. "Look at my Little Ballerina, learning how to give head like it's the eighties."

"What happened in the eighties?" I asked, feeling ridiculously stupid. You'd think I know more about the decade than he did. He shrugged.

"Nothing. People liked giving head, I guess."

I shook my head on a laugh. He was so ridiculous sometimes, but that's exactly what made it so easy to unwind with this guy. I flattened my palm against his chest. "I need to ask you something."

"Uh-oh. Am I in trouble, Ms. Greene? Have I been a bad boy? Do I need a spanking?" He wiggled his brows and laughed.

God, he was sexy. And God, it was creepy.

I shook my head, closing my eyes so I wouldn't see his reaction to my blush. "Tell me about Defy," I said.

None of the teachers knew much about Defy, other than the injuries we spotted on Monday mornings. Students got into bloody fights at Vicious's parties, and there was nothing we could do about it.

Jaime frowned. "What do you want to know?"

"I want to know everything." I cleared my throat. "Where, why, how, and most of all…why are *you* doing it?"

His eyes darkened, and he pulled his blond hair into a high bun. I watched him silently, swallowing hard while he examined me under his lashes. I was stepping deeper into a territory that wasn't mine. We both were. This was intimate and secretive, two lines we promised we wouldn't cross outside the bedroom.

Are we breaking the rules?

It occurred to me that I was the first one to step over the line that I was so quick to paint in our relationship. But it also occurred to me that there wasn't one line. It was more like an abstract painting full of lines, circles and triangles. It was a mess, and trying to maneuver your moves in this thing between us was hopeless.

"This doesn't leave this room," Jaime warned, dipping his chin down, his nose touching mine.

"Of course," I said as if this was obvious. We were still on the floor, my legs knotted with his. I wanted to toss aside my teacher hat at that moment. To burn it to ashes, more like. "This is between you and me. I'm just curious."

"Well…" He pulled me deeper between his legs, opening them wider to accommodate me. His eyes honed on an invisible spot on the wall. This was hard for him. Giving up a secret that wasn't wholly his. "Where? At Vicious's place. Every weekend. Guys know better than to come to his parties if they don't feel like fighting. And still…everyone does. Let's admit it. This town is fucking boring. We're all rich, privileged, and desperate to fill in the void."

"What void?"

"*That* void. Whether it's sex or pressure or money. We fight on the tennis court. His father and stepmother never use it, so they never notice the blood stains, which their handyman takes care of during the week."

That void was familiar. I didn't want to tell him that I had it, too. The hole in my soul. And that I, too, found a way to fill it. *With him.*

Suddenly, he snaked one hand behind my back and lowered me along with him to the floor, doing it slowly so I wouldn't hit my head.

A wicked grin curved his lips. "Why? Because it's fun. Because men have become so fucking emasculated by society, we sometimes feel like having our balls back. Why do dudes love *Fight Club* so much? It's because behind every A&F boxers-wearing guy who smells like citrus aftershave and knows who Versace is and takes you out on a date to an Italian dinner and a foreign film, there's a savage who just wants to grab you by the hair and drag you to his cave."

His other hand moved between us, sliding down my belly, finding my soaking panties. I was wearing a knee-length dress, but it was flipped up and Jaime didn't look like he was bothered by it too much. He rubbed my entrance through my panties furiously.

"How? Someone steps out to the pool with his sleeves rolled up. That's an invitation to fight. You can't challenge a specific guy. The other guy has to volunteer. Chicks dig it, even when you lose, so guys do it, because pussy is nice, even when you have a bleeding lip. We use our fists. Kicks. Basic MMA shit. But we fight clean, mostly. And if things get out of hand, which they usually don't unless Vicious's involved..." He bit my lip, tugging my underwear down roughly and pushing in two fingers. "Then one of the HotHoles breaks it off before shit goes to the ER."

I whimpered, tightening around him. He was rougher than

usual, and I doubted it was a coincidence. He wanted to show me that he was a man, not a kid.

And he succeeded. In and out, in and out, he fingered me while I writhed on my kitchen floor underneath him.

So this was it. This was Defy. I had more questions I couldn't exactly articulate at that moment, but one thing was clear—Jaime wasn't afraid of getting hurt. Not physically, anyway.

But what about emotionally?

And what about me? Would I be able to take the hit when things between us went south?

All I knew was that *my* south liked him. So much so, that I came on his fingers before he even had the chance to touch my clit.

"You feel pretty manly to me," I breathed out, all jelly-legged with half-mast eyes.

"And you feel like a woman worthy of a fight, Ms. Greene."

Chapter Nine

S IX HEAVENLY WEEKS TICKED BY before Jaime claimed not only my body, but my heart. Unsurprisingly, it was the day I got my period (AKA the time when my hormones were wreaking havoc with my body). It was also the day that I moved.

I'd found a place in a small beach town on the outskirts of Todos Santos, and I'd arranged for a substitute teacher to cover my classes that day. That didn't stop Principal Followhill from grunting that I had some nerve taking time off when my position was on the line and my classes were behind schedule on the required syllabus. She was back to her old ways now that she'd paid me off for Jaime's car accident.

Since I didn't want to spend much money on movers, I'd decided to do some of the heavy lifting myself. I spent my morning running from my old apartment to the new one, moving boxes up and down the stairs. I was sweaty and smelly, with my messy pony-tail, PINK black sweatpants, and a yellow tank top that showed off my toned midriff. If there was a potential husband waiting for me in the dingy complex I was moving into, he was going to think that I was hot. And possibly homeless.

On my third run back to my old apartment, I saw Jaime

waiting at my door. He was wearing a white sleeveless tank and khaki shorts. The kind that hugged his ass as if to say, *You better believe I'm touching this all day, bitch.*

My heart fluttered in my chest, which made my soul lurch in pain. *Just until school ends, remember?*

"You're supposed to be at school." I slipped past him, marching into my apartment. Yes, I was cold to him because of his mother's behavior yesterday, and no, it was not fair, but I couldn't help it. I was on my period. He needed to cut me some slack here. Besides—he really was skipping school. I still cared about his education. A lot, actually.

"I thought you were sick." He hurried into my apartment before the door shut behind me, his hands tucked in his pockets. "You didn't even mention you were moving today when we saw each other yesterday."

"You saw the boxes."

"Yeah. They have been sitting around since the first time I was here. You never put anything in them. I thought you were moving in, not out. What kind of bullshit is this?"

"My landlord wants the place for himself, so I got a new one." I shrugged and refused to explain more because this thing with him was supposed to be fun. He didn't need to know my schedule, even though most days, we both knew exactly where the other person was. There was pain in his voice. I not only heard it, I felt it. Like a punch to my stomach. This was wrong. He needed to know, we owed each other nothing.

With a sigh, Jaime dropped the subject. "Whatever. Let's hang out."

"You can't skip classes, Jaime. You'll fail. Even if you've already been accepted to college, it looks bad." I started gathering my clothes by their hangers. I was going to carry some more boxes to my car but didn't want him to see me melting into a sweaty pile of PMS rage.

"In other words, you don't wanna hang out with me?" He followed me, knocking over a stack of boxes with his huge body in the process.

"No. I don't have time to fuck around today." I kept walking back and forth, stuffing my hanging clothes into a pair of laundry baskets, hoping he'd get the hint.

Damn him. It was his fault I wasn't packed already in the first place.

Jaime grabbed my stiff shoulder, studying me. "You think that's why I came here? To fuck you?"

His raw gaze alone stripped off a layer of my shitty attitude, but I still needed him to leave. This had to stop. *We* had to stop.

Then why did I run out of breath every time I thought about my life without him?

I shrugged again. "No? Okay, no then. Still, I'm moving, as you can see, and I've got my hands full." I lifted up the heap of clothes in my hands for emphasis. "See you tomorrow."

"I'll help," Jaime announced, grabbing the biggest, heaviest box and throwing it up on one of his shoulders.

I wanted to protest, but shit, that box was like a hundred pounds, easy. I was avoiding the thing like it was that drunk aunt at a wedding reception no one wanted to talk to. Scanning the prominent veins in his arms popping out, I knew I should decline his help. He should be in school. It could even raise suspicion, me and him not showing up on the same day. I remembered Vicious's veiled threat.

But…I really needed the help.

Also, I was helpless when it came to him.

"Right," I said after a pause. "I'll show you where I'm parked."

He tutted with a growl, reminding me who the boss around here is. "Makes more sense to use the Range Rover. More space. We can finish sooner. It'll leave us more time for ourselves."

I exhaled, climbing down the stairs. "Just to give you a heads-up—I'm on my period."

"You don't say. You hid it so well." He threw the box into the back of his SUV like it was feather-light. "Like I said, I'm here to hang out." He speared me with his scowl.

I guess we were hanging out.

We finished moving (and unpacking) everything by seven that night, and Jaime made a quick run to the nearest Wendy's. He asked if he should pick up beer too, and after I said sure, I nearly bit off my tongue, realizing what I'd done. It was easy to forget he wasn't my age. Funny thing was, he *did* bring beer. When I asked him if he had a fake ID, he chuckled and mussed my hair like I was an adorable kid, explaining that the HotHoles never got carded in Todos Santos. I shook my head and cracked open my beer.

Jaime hooked up my TV and dragged the coffee table to the middle of the room. We watched a shitty game show from the 80s. His feet were on the table, while I curled up on the sofa. We looked like a couple. What's more—we acted like one.

It felt natural. And scary. For a moment, just a brief, crazy, I-obviously-need-help moment, I imagined that we were moving into this apartment together, me and him.

"How did we get to this point? Holy shit, I'm fucking my student," I mumbled out of nowhere, my eyes still glued to the TV.

"Well…" Jaime stretched, downing what was left of his beer in one swig and slamming it against the table. "I blackmailed you into it. That's how."

His sarcasm held a lie I wanted to believe. We both knew he hadn't forced me. I fucked him by choice. I put the beer to my lips, stalling.

"Okay." He licked his lips and turned off the TV, rubbing his thighs. "Let's play Truth or Dare."

I was tempted to remind him I wasn't twelve but didn't want

to be even more of a grouch. So, I batted my eyelashes innocently. "Are you going to milk my secrets out of me?"

"Might as well since you aren't going to milk the jizz out of me tonight." He got up from the couch, disappeared into my tiny new kitchen, and returned with a bottle of Jose Cuervo. Holding the bottle of tequila by its neck, he slouched back down beside me. Now we were both sitting cross-legged on the sofa, facing each other. A fan hummed above us, and if we were really silent—which we were—we could hear the sound of the waves crashing against the shore, their rhythm systematic, like a sweet lullaby.

"This conversation needs booze, so a shot for every time we choose a truth over a dare." Jaime rested the bottle between us, his voice clipped. He was looking at me funny.

Jaime was normally impossible to read. A hot, carefree jock with darkness behind his light eyes, but the expression he wore...it was borderline pained.

"I don't want you drinking under my roof. You're under twenty-one."

"I'm eighteen. Any other place in the world—virtually all over Europe—I'd be allowed to get shitfaced wherever I want."

"We're not in Europe," I deadpanned.

"We will be, one day. Together," his bizarre statement came out so confident. I almost doubled over. Okay, then. Back to the subject, I guess.

"I'm a daredevil." I cocked a brow, laughing mainly to hide my embarrassment at how nervous I was.

"Real daredevils choose the truth. It's always more challenging than a dare." His right eye ticked. "So...truth or dare?"

"Dare," I teased, hoping to lighten the tension. Wherever this conversation was leading, it was going to be a raw, dangerous place for the both of us.

Jaime dipped his chin down and ran his thumb over his lower

lip, his playful-self peeking from the wall of graveness he had built around him tonight. "I dare you to look me in the eye and tell me you don't have feelings for me."

His words were simple, yet his request—impossible.

I blinked, realizing for the first time that the answer to his question was something I wasn't ready to face. "Truth," I said and swallowed painfully.

Jaime tipped his head back and laughed. It sounded gruff and unhappy.

I looked away, feeling my face whitening. "What? I'm allowed to change my mind."

"You're not." He reached for me, brushing his thumb over my cheek. "Tell me what you feel." His tone had changed to cushion-soft.

"Why?" I whispered, resisting the urge to close my eyes. If I did, a tear would escape. I never cried. Not since the accident in NY. I dealt. Damn you, Jaime Followhill. I dealt.

Jaime thumbed my chin, tilting my face to meet his gaze. Slowly, he brought his forehead to mine and closed his eyes, releasing a defeated breath. "Because I feel it, too."

I wanted him to kiss me. To kiss me hard and soft all at once, a kiss that'd assure me that I wasn't crazy for discovering what I'd just discovered on this tattered sofa in this tiny apartment.

That I was in love with my student.

I'd tried to convince myself that it was just sex. It wasn't. It was pizza nights and laughing under my cheap, itchy blanket and nicknaming each other stupid names. I was Little Ballerina, while he was Giraffe Tongue, for reasons that gave me countless orgasms.

It was watching Tarantino movies and stealing breathless kisses at school, two thieves of pleasure, begging to confess their crime. I was spellbound, desperate, and possessed. And I knew with certainty that once he graduated and moved away for college, the blow would be just as hard as my subway accident.

Dancing *was* my life.

But Jaime? Jaime *is* my life, I realized.

He took a swig of the tequila, screwed the top back on, and jerked me into him, holding the back of my neck to bring my lips to his.

"Ask me." His alcohol-fumed breath oozed into my mouth.

"Truth or dare?"

"Truth. And it's gonna be ugly. Buckle up." He let me go, pushing away, his eyes fluttering shut. Frustration and hurt radiated from his face, and he slouched on the couch, looking almost defeated. This was not the Jaime I knew. The devil with the panty-dropping smile.

Worry gnawed at my gut.

"The first time I saw you," he began, "I wanted to slap my name on your ass, let everyone know that I was going to be the only guy to tap that shit. You looked like a princess, Mel. An insanely hot princess with a perfect posture and unruly curls." He smirked. "'Course, acting on it was out of the question. A fantasy. Then I came home that first day of my senior year, and Mom wouldn't shut up about you. *Melody this and Melody that.* How bad you were at your job, how you were gonna ruin Mr. Pitterman's legacy, blah blah, bullshit blah. She hated your guts. Gave you the job only because he croaked so suddenly."

He was telling me things that I already knew, but it didn't make them any less painful. The previous Lit teacher had died of a heart attack two days before school started. Principal Followhill had needed to act fast.

"You became a favorite topic at our dinner table. She loathed your ass." Jaime took a sip, wincing from the bite of the tequila. "You were pretty and young and completely unimpressed by her power and the status and stinking money that runs our fucked-up little town." He spoke with his eyes squeezed shut. Embarrassed, probably for the first time in his life. "You were a good teacher. That's why I never gave you shit. It wasn't your fault we were a bunch of privileged assholes."

I placed my hand on his arm. He drank some more.

Your pain is mine, and I want to shoulder it, because I can. Because that's what I do. I carry my pain all the time. Let me take away yours, my touch begged him.

"I told Mom to shut her trap numerous times. Not because I wanted to defend you but because gossiping about you was feeding a monster inside me. Talking about you only made it harder for me to ignore you. So fucking hot..." He nodded his head and bit his full lip, eyes still closed. "When I heard how you had to drop out of Julliard, I wanted to die for you. I had a feeling teaching wasn't your calling. I kept thinking about eighteen-year-old you. My age. Your heart broken by bad luck, shattered by an accident that'd left more than a physical scar."

I shifted on my small couch. It felt smaller with every word he said. My gaze traveled down to my hands. I was flattered. I was horrified. But most of all, I was confused. "You were thinking about me for the whole year?"

He snorted a sad laugh.

"More than thinking. Six weeks after school started, I had a huge fight with my mom. Coach Rowland was giving Trent shit about breaking his ankle. Like he planned to get hurt and fuck-up his whole football future. We finally stood up for Trent against Coach, but Mom defended Rowland. My fight with her left me so frustrated I gave in to my weakness for you. I followed you to your apartment, tried to steal a private peek through your bedroom window. I don't know why I did that. It was like drinking fucking Emergen-C. I just wanted to take the edge off."

Jaime opened his eyes, his blues challenging me. "You were the perfect sin to commit, Melody. Begging to be taken. Untouched by the rest of Todos Santos's posing and entitlement. I got hooked. From that day on, I followed you everywhere like an eager puppy. To the supermarket, the gas station…the fucking park every morning before practice, where I watched you doing yoga positions and tried not to rub a quick one out behind a tree. I followed you on blind dates, and when I realized you'd never met the idiots before, I also found your dating account and opened a profile under a fake name just so I could stalk you better."

My hand shook as I slapped it over my mouth. None of this sounded like the guy I'd dated. I mean, screwed. No, wait, dated. Definitely dated. In the last ten minutes, this relationship had moved faster than a sprinter at an all-you-can-eat pasta buffet.

Another swig. Another deep breathe. Another thorn in my heart.

Jaime was treading closer to shitfaced territory with every truth that rolled out of his mouth.

"I'm listening," I prompted, afraid that he'd clam up on me.

"Three months ago, I caught my mother cheating on my father with Coach Rowland. In my bed."

I wheezed. We were running barefoot in a minefield of emotions, and Jaime had just exploded an IED under my legs.

Jaime's dad had never bothered to hop on the gossip train traveling through Todos Santos. I didn't know much about him. Only that he was known as a philanthropist who worked with several big charities, and that despite his privileged lineage, he wasn't too interested in glitz and glamor.

"I don't know which part was worse. That she let Coach emotionally abuse Trent for years or that she was fucking the bastard in my bed. I'd like to believe the location was just convenient. My bed always smelled like sex anyway and was never made." His eyes glistened with pain.

I wrapped my hands around his neck.

Jaime spoke into my hair, his chin pressed to my shoulder. "Fucking someone who she hated sounded like good therapy. So I started planning, and you and I began talking more on that dating site. You opened up to me. Told me what you liked and disliked. Your taste in music. Favorite movies. Dream vacations, layer after layer peeled. And when it was time to strike—I set up a date. I was the loser guy who still lived with his mom at twenty-six."

Bastard.

I laughed. He laughed. Then I grew silent and started crying. Damn PMS. He wiped my cheeks and offered me the tequila. I snatched it from him and took a swig. Everything was a mess.

"You're a real asshole, Jaime."

Jaime rubbed his head, mussing his glorious man-bun. "The text message you got when you backed out of your parking space? Planned. The reason you bumped into me? I set you up, Mel. The text was a deliberate distraction. A trap. But you know what the worst part is?"

I shook my head, feeling my tears, hot and angry, running down my face.

He stared at me through red-rimmed eyes. He didn't shed tears, but I knew that he was holding them back. "Somewhere between the quest of wanting to fuck you and secretly rebelling against my mom, I fell in love with you. It wasn't a beautiful process. Hell..." He laughed, rubbing the back of his neck. "It wasn't even romantic. But it happened. Because you're strong but vulnerable. Witty as fuck but not bitter or deliberately mean. Because I had to chase your ass to nail you down, and you still keep me on my toes. But if we're going to keep going on like this, where I have to convince you to give me the time of the day while you look over your shoulder, constantly trying to shake me off, I need to bail out of this before I get hurt."

He took my cheeks and dragged my face to meet his. "Men with big cocks have fragile hearts. You know the saying: big cock, big heart. Well, I'm proof it's true."

I let out a breathless chuckle. Our noses brushed, and I sucked in a breath. A moment of silence ticked by.

"So…are you mine, Melody?"

Was I? Yeah. Without a shadow of a doubt, I was. God, were we really going to do this?

I nodded, sniffing my runny nose. "No one else's." I pursed my lips, already tasting the saltiness of the grief that accompanied this statement.

Our lips crushed together, needy and demanding. I wasn't mad. I wasn't freaked out. For the first time in ages I was just… content.

A foreign feeling I wanted more of. A drug I would later get addicted to.

"You need to go back to dancing," Jaime said through noisy, sloppy kisses. "Your leg's fine now."

"I'm twenty-six." I sniffed, more tears falling, but we were still kissing. "That's one-hundred-and-eighty-two in dog years and, like, two-hundred-and-two in ballerina years."

"Then settle for something outside of a ballet company, granny. *Teach*."

Finally, I pulled away from his face, sucking in a breath. I tapped my lower lip. "The dance studio here is owned by a friend of your mother."

"So find a studio in San Diego. It's only a thirty-minute drive. You can fulfill your dream and still live close to me."

Whoa, what? This caught me off guard. My eyebrows knitted, and I searched his face. "Jaime, you're moving to Texas. You're going to college there. You have a great future planned."

He held my gaze, ignoring my words completely. "You could

even teach ballet in LA. Vicious is going to college there. If he can get in, so can I."

I wondered if he was drunk or just crazy. He sounded like both. "Vicious isn't the greatest role model. He's just taking a little break until he burns this town down. You and I both know that."

Jaime shook his head, a sad smile on his face. "Even if he does, I'd help him light the match. The HotHoles stick together. That's who we are." He laced his fingers through mine.

"You're not staying here," I stated. Even though, selfishly, I didn't want him to move away. Moreover, the very thought of him living in Texas, far away from me, made my skin crawl.

"Bull. Shit. I'm staying where the only people I care about are. You. Vicious. Trent. Dean might even be staying if Vicious doesn't kill him…" He broke off.

"In Defy?" I prodded.

"Not that. It's more complicated."

I shook my head. As much as I liked having him around, it was in his best interest to leave. This place was hell. The city of saints was filled with nothing but sinners. He'd already been corrupted but not beyond repair.

"No." I made my voice firmer, trying to use that authoritative teacher tone my parents were so good at. "You said you loved me. If you do, then promise me, you'll leave here before you get hurt. And no more Defy." *People have probably already been hurt*, I thought. "Go away, James."

"Can't." He brought my hands to his lips, kissing my knuckles one by one. "I'm not leaving you here or anywhere else. Hey, I never wanted to go to college in Texas anyway. You know how dangerous it is to look this good on a campus that big? I could get fucking roofied, Ms. G."

He winked. I laughed, but it died quickly.

"Then at least promise me you'll keep Vicious away from

Millie?" I sighed. I wanted her safe, for the same reason I wanted me to be safe. She was my mini-me. Before I was broken, anyway.

"He'll never stay away from her." Jaime's expression grew tight. "For one, he wants to ruin her. And two? She lives too close. Her parents work for the Spencers."

I'd suspected she was the complication he mentioned, and now he'd confirmed it. She was a good distraction for us too. This wasn't the right time to talk about our plans as a couple. Jaime was too drunk. Too emotional to think clearly.

We both were.

But deep down, my truths were already starting to dig their way out of my layers of indifference. And they told me it wasn't about the alcohol, or the late hour, or the inconvenient talks about the future.

It was about us. It *was* us.

Chapter Ten

THE NEXT DAY, I WOKE up different.

I don't know how it happened, but it did, and it was all Jaime's fault. That emptiness that swirled in my gut like a storm, refusing to calm down despite my best efforts? It wasn't there the next day.

After the accident that ended my studying at Julliard, I thought I'd never escape that empty feeling. Surely, when your future career and dreams consumed you, chased you around, like bitter memories that nipped at your skin every time you saw a picture of a ballerina or heard about a traveling company in town, you couldn't come back from it and find something else to fill the void.

That void.

Logically, I'd assumed that I was probably going to meet a guy. Get married. Start a life. I still had things to do and accomplish, and some of them might even be fun. I thought that maybe, I'd find my calling elsewhere. Not teaching high school Lit, but maybe with my kids? I could probably be a good mom. A soccer mom. Live through my children.

But the next morning, when I woke up in the arms of my student, he didn't feel like my student. He felt like my mentor. Like a man who knows the way to that slippery, elusive thing called happiness.

Not just physically. The way his hard muscles and long body enveloped me. The fact that he was so tall and wide, made me feel protected and cherished. It was his warmth—not the one from his skin, the one from who he was—that filled me with something that wasn't emptiness.

"This is the part where you run away from this, Mel," he whispered into my ear, his morning voice gruff and his morning wood hard against my lower back. We were spooning, and I couldn't smell his morning breath, but I bet it wasn't as bad as the average person's. The guy was just annoyingly perfect.

"Run, Ms. Greene. As fast as you'd like. I'm going to catch you, and I'm going to have fun showing you that there's no escape from this."

I rolled around to face him, the space between us warm from sleeping together in my new place. I grinned, a smile that wasn't controlled or calculated.

He yanked my hand from under the covers and pressed my fingers to his full lips. "Shit, Ms. Greene got brave."

"I'm about to get braver and offer you breakfast." I didn't know what I was saying or why I was saying it, but I knew I didn't want him gone. Not yet.

"You literally have nothing other than alcohol." Jaime laughed a throaty laugh, the type that left your mouth after you'd had a long night of sleep.

"I'll go out and get some groceries. You wait here." I gave him half a shrug.

"Or here's a better idea. I'll take you out to a local diner. Now what do you think?" He grabbed my waist and jerked me into his hot body, pressing his erection between my thighs.

I sighed, my teeth sinking into my bottom lip until I almost bled. How could I be so sexually frustrated every time he wasn't inside me? We'd obviously had a lot of sex.

"I think you're insane. People could spot us."

"We'll go somewhere outside of town. Maybe by the highway. Stop being so paranoid. Todos Santos is full of old, rich white people. They don't venture farther than the city limits without a good reason. They're too scared of the unwashed masses in the outside world."

I let out a small chuckle. He was right, of course.

"We're playing a dangerous game here, Jaime," I warned.

"I don't know any other way to play it."

Another month ticked by. My relationship with Jaime became alarmingly intimate. He moved most of his stuff to my place and slept-over ninety percent of the time. I couldn't tell him no after he'd confided in me about his mom and Coach Rowland. I didn't know many people who'd be eager to sleep on the same bed their mom used to cheat on her husband. But while we were enjoying more sex, more phone calls, more pizza nights, and more talks about our uncertain future, more, more, *more*—it was becoming evident that we were starting to raise people's eyebrows.

Vicious caught us red-handed, making out while hidden behind Jaime's SUV at Liberty Park after a midnight walk. (We only went out together when everyone else was fast asleep). Vicious didn't look surprised. Just offered us his usual scowl, growling about how we grossed him out and moved on, probably looking for a victim to murder that night. He kept his mouth shut.

But other people didn't. At school, girls were getting restless. Jaime wouldn't give them the time of day, and while he made up something about a girlfriend who lived in LA, nobody believed him. This HotHole in a steady relationship? A long distance one, too? *Pfft.* Yeah, right.

One day, a cheerleader named Kadence went as far as following Jaime back to my apartment and reported back to the masses that he'd rented his own place. I was just glad that she didn't know the place was mine and that school was going to be over in few weeks.

But it was all too good to be true. The last week of school, I found that out.

It started with the innocent sound of a text message pinging in the dark, followed by an announcement.

"I'm going out," Jaime said.

It was half past midnight, and we were both snuggled up in bed. His mom thought he had moved in with Vicious, and Spencer confirmed the lie. Shockingly, his father and stepmother did, too. This kid *did* rule everything around him, his parents included.

"Where to?" I breathed more of him into me, still clutching his waist. He got up, sat on the bed, and fired off a text message, avoiding eye contact.

"Don't." His voice was rough. Clipped.

I scooted up in bed, frowning. "Jaime, what's up?"

He groaned, pulling on a white tee over his bare chest. No matter how many times I've seen him naked, it always made me feel a little sad when he covered those great abs. "Nothing's up. Last time I checked, it's not against the law to go hang out with your friends."

He had yet to look at me.

"Yeah." I grabbed his arm, prompting him to look at me. "But it is against the law to do half the shit Vicious makes you guys do. So it is my business."

"Actually"—he shook out of my touch, turning around and smiling tightly—"that's exactly why you aren't going to get shit from me. It'd only drag you into a pile of crap I'm not willing to pull you into. I'll be back later." He kissed my temple. "If you need anything, text."

"You've been Defied," I said dryly.

He ignored me, squatting down and tying his shoelaces.

"Vicious wants you to do something for him, huh?"

"Don't worry."

Like hell. "I'm nothing *but* worried," I gritted.

Petrified would be a better word to describe my feelings in that moment. Vicious always came up with stupid shit, and the HotHoles always played his dangerous games.

Watching him walk away stirred something in me I thought didn't exist anymore. Anger. Rage. Curiosity. I was tired of being led. Into relationships. Into situations. Tired of accepting everything that was handed to me—my broken dream, broken leg, half-assed career and the job I hated.

I sat in bed, alert. I heard the silent engine of the Range Rover purring outside, and that was my cue.

I slipped into my dented Ford and followed his vehicle all the way to the beach.

Chapter Eleven

T HERE WAS NO WAY I would be able to hide my car in the deserted parking area overlooking the marina, so I parked at a gas station on Main Street, near the water, and bolted straight into a convenience store. Its windows faced where Jaime had parked his Range Rover. A bell chimed above my head as I entered the deserted store, and faint Indian music greeted me from a staticky radio. A beautiful girl with long black hair smiled from behind the cash register, her gaze returning to her book. Hiding inside the convenience store allowed me to watch him without being caught. Considering Jaime was no stranger to stalking, I tried to downplay my actions, internally justifying myself.

My boyfriend left in the middle of the night without any explanation. I deserve answers.

I watched Jaime's large body through the glass door, jogging across the parking lot, as he approached Trent and Dean on the edge of the piers at the marina. They slapped each other's backs, talking animatedly before Jaime broke the circle. Then they strode up the wooden piers where all the famous yachts of Todos Santos were docked.

The penny dropped and with it, my heart. It wasn't a Defy

fight. It was retaliation. It was cooking up revenge and making bad people pay.

Rowland.

The Rowlands had a restaurant on a big-ass boat, one of the most luxurious in SoCal, docked along one of the piers. It was their pride, joy, and main source of income. Hence, it was the sweet spot the HotHoles probably wanted to crush and eliminate from the earth.

Storming out of the convenience store, I ran toward the marina fast enough to leave a trail of smoke behind.

I wasn't completely opposed to Jaime staying in Todos Santos. The selfish (AKA the biggest) part of my personality wanted him to stick around. I loved him and wanted to make gorgeous babies with him. (I wasn't crazy enough to utter this aloud. Then again, he was my stalker, so Crazy was a language we were both fluent in.) But it was a whole different ball game—letting him do something insane that could permanently screw up his life. Even Baron Spencer and his peeps weren't above the law when it came to serious crimes.

And Vicious took his revenge very. Fucking. Seriously.

I ran across the skaters' ramp overlooking the marina and crept up the pier between two giant yachts. One of them belonged to the Spencers—*Marie,* after Vicious's late mother—and the other belonged to a Saudi tycoon who had a summerhouse in Todos Santos but never actually bothered to drop by. It allowed me a good angle on the boys, who, just as I suspected, stopped in front of *La Belle,* the Rowlands' boat and exclusive restaurant.

Trent fisted a five-gallon gasoline can while Dean spoke on the phone, his voice inaudible to me. Jaime produced his cell and looked to be typing up a text. A few moments later, my cell vibrated in my pocket. Luckily, I'd silenced it before I got here.

Jaime:
Crashing @ Vic's 2nite. Don't wait up.

Fury flowed through my veins, sizzling and consuming. I knew why they were doing it. Jaime hated Coach Rowland for fucking his mom. Trent hated Coach Rowland for laughing when he broke his ankle during football season and his son for breaking it a second time. Vicious…he just hated everyone in general. And Dean? Dean looked like he loved everything and everyone in life, the player with the big, genuine smile, but I saw him. Saw below the perfect, shiny exterior. And what I saw wasn't pretty. Not by a long shot.

Regardless to how each of them viewed the retaliation, the HotHoles were like brothers. The re-injury to Trent's ankle—like my fall in the subway—was the final kiss of death to his football career. Someone had to pay for greasing the locker room floor.

The Rowlands' money was the price.

The HotHoles waited on the pier beside *La Belle* until Vicious appeared at the top of the stairs leading down from the parking lot to the marina.

He wasn't alone.

Toby Rowland—gagged, bound by the wrists and sweating like a slut in an STD clinic—was standing next to him. There was a kidney-shaped urine stain over his groin. He didn't struggle, just glared at the ground, weeping silently.

Vicious was in full asshole mode that night. He descended the stairs behind Rowland, pushing him one stair at a time, beaming like a groom on his wedding day. The marina was well lit, so it wasn't hard to catch him cracking his neck, his biceps flexing in anticipation.

"Look who's decided to join us." His voice was low, taunting. It sent chills down my spine. I sometimes wondered if Vicious's parents conceived him on Hitler's tombstone or if his mom had a freak accident involving poison and voodoo while she was pregnant. He was too scary for a teenager. Too dangerous for someone who grew up in pretentious luxury. *Too dead for a living human.*

Rowland and Vicious stopped at the last stair, where Vicious pushed him headfirst to fall to the pier. Toby winced into the gag in his mouth, coughing. Jaime and Dean picked him up and tore the cloth from his face.

"Oh, man, your mouth is bleeding. Here, let me help." Jaime's hand reached toward Toby's face before he swung his arm back, throwing a punch from hell right into his nose.

Toby's head flew backward, landing against Vicious's chest.

Vicious clasped Toby's arms, hissing into his ear almost erotically, "Don't worry, I got you. I won't let them hurt you. No. I'm planning to do all the hurting myself."

Trent stepped forward and blocked my view with his broad back. All I saw was the three HotHoles' backs. Vicious and Toby were well-hidden behind the other guys.

I heard Toby crying and whimpering, clomping his feet, begging, wailing, trying to break free. Then Dean stepped aside, allowing me a first glimpse at Rowland's new face.

Bloated.

Bleeding.

Destroyed.

Seeing the welts—smelling the blood—in person, felt so much worse than looking at it on a Monday morning. The four HotHoles were so troubled. Each had their own reason to be. I knew what ate Jaime…but I didn't know why the others were so hell-bent on feeding and consuming so much pain.

Jaime was now grasping Toby's hair while he was on his knees. Vicious slouched down to sit on a step, lighting a cigarette nonchalantly and pointing his Zippo at *La Belle*. His knuckles dripped blood, and his pale cheeks were flushed pink. Yet when he opened his mouth, calmness flowed out with every word.

"Nice boat your parents have. How many years have they put into that floating banquet room? Mom used to say your pasta tasted like stale balls."

Toby sighed in defeat, barely shaking his head, while Dean and Trent laughed.

"Okay, you're right. She didn't really say that. She wouldn't have known what stale balls taste like. But your mom does, right? Rowland is a nasty piece of fuck."

I was sure I saw Jaime's face twitch, but maybe it was because I was privy to his secret.

"Last words before we burn this beauty down?" Vicious puffed smoke, toying with his lighter.

"Please," Toby sniffed and coughed. "Just…please."

"You ruined my career," Trent said through a clenched jaw, fists tightening. "And didn't give me the option to beg for my leg before you greased the locker room floor. Was it your dad's idea? Or did he just look the other way?"

"So s-s-s-sorry." Toby's words were drenched with red saliva.

Vicious stood up, slapping Trent's shoulder. "The kid says that he's sorry. Does that cut it?"

Trent shook his head slowly, eyes trained on Toby. Vicious swiveled to Rowland and shrugged. "Apparently, sorry isn't gonna do it. Guess we're back to plan A."

Trent took a long stride toward *La Belle*, unscrewed the cap on the five-gallon can, and climbed the steps leading up to the yacht and the restaurant inside. The stench of gasoline filled the air. Vicious still played with his Zippo, thumbing it teasingly.

Light.

Out.

Light.

Out.

Light...

Normally the marina was patrolled regularly. I had no doubt the HotHoles had something to do with the absence of security. Trent poured gasoline from the restaurant's entry door along the wooden deck and back down the steps to the marina in a fuse-like line. After he threw the empty gas can into the water, he walked to Vicious's side and planted a hand on his shoulder with a little nod. This was Baron Spencer's cue.

"Goodbye, *La Belle*. You'll be missed...but not by us." Vicious chuckled darkly, flipping the lit Zippo toward the trail of gasoline.

A whoosh of flames erupted. Fire raced up the steps and across the deck to the restaurant door.

"Let's go!"

The boys turned around, holding Toby like a prisoner in both arms, and dragged him back to the parking lot. They made sure his face was toward the marina so he could see the destruction of his family's most precious possession. Flames leaped high, and black smoke engulfed the yacht in a choking hug.

I had to escape. To turn around and run away.

Why didn't you stop them, Mel? I knew the answer to that one. The retaliation was justified. The Rowlands deserved the HotHoles' wrath.

Running up the stairs, hysteria taking over my body as the heat of the fire licked at my legs, I heard the *clank* of something dropping behind me. I didn't have time to pick it up. Not even to turn around and check what it was. I fled the scene and bolted back to my apartment.

I locked the door. Twice. Took inventory: keys, phone, and purse.

They were all there.

I sighed in relief and dragged my body down, my back against the door.

Safe. For now.

But then it occurred to me that I didn't care about my safety. Not as much as I cared about his.

I wasn't supposed to know where he was that night, but I couldn't help but text him, just to check that he's okay.

Me:
Are you guys having fun?

Jaime:
You bet we are. But I can't stop thinking about you.

Me:
Is that why you left without explaining?

Jaime:
Yes, Mel. That's exactly why I left without explaining. Because I think about you before I think about myself. Always remember that, Little Ballerina. Always.

Chapter Twelve

"**M**s. Greene. My office. Now."

Principal Followhill's face was thunder about to crack, and I knew she'd be unleashing a shit-storm on me the minute I stepped into her office. It didn't matter. It was only yesterday that I'd witnessed her son—my boyfriend—committing a serious crime. This was the last week of school, and I'd already started applying for positions at nearby schools for next year. She had no power over me anymore.

Or so I thought.

I walked into her office and closed the door, silently taking a seat.

"Straight to the point?" She leaned over her table, legs crossed. "Give me one good reason why I shouldn't call the cops and have you arrested right here on the premises."

My heart stopped, just like that. *What?*

"Excuse me?" My eyebrows shot up. My pulse vibrated be-tween my ears.

Followhill tapped her shiny fingernail on her desk and shot me an insincere smile. "Let me refresh your memory—big fire. Burnt yacht. A devastated family. All happened yesterday. Now, again,

Ms. Greene…" She leaned closer to me, whispering, "Give me one good reason not to call our beloved police chief?"

I took a deep breath, closing my eyes to gain strength. "Reason number one? Because I didn't do shit."

"Mr. Rowland and his son, Toby, don't seem to think so. They say you set fire to *La Belle* last night. Wanting to get back at the school's staff before you leave here. The family's restaurant is ruined." She cocked her head sideways, a smug smile spreading on her face.

Panic exploded in my veins, and my head became a jumbled mess of incoherent thoughts. I had so much to say and nothing at all to utter, all at the same time, so I settled for, "Huh?"

"I was skeptical, too, at first. I said why would she? But then there was evidence." She slid her drawer open, producing a necklace. *My necklace.* Shit. That's what I dropped when I ran away last night. The silver anchor glittered between her fingers.

She tossed it to me, shaking her head. "And a motive, too. I suppose you've heard Coach Rowland's sister, Chelsea, is going to take your position next year."

Actually, I had no idea, and I can't say I cared much, either. At this point, I wouldn't have stayed in the job even if she'd offered me a seven-digit salary.

"Is that all you got?" I murmured, folding my arms over my chest. "People are still allowed to take a stroll in your town's precious marina. Doesn't make them guilty of burning down random yachts."

"Toby gave it to me this morning. He swears he saw you doing it."

I'd had it. I bolted up out of my chair and stared her down. "You know *exactly* who did it." Rage consumed every inch of my body, and I banged my fist against her desk. "And I get the feeling you know why, too. This is blackmail." My lips twitched. "Twice in one semester," I added.

Principal Followhill stood up slowly, staring me in the eye. "You think I don't know you're sleeping with my son? Eyeing his fortune, his money, *his future*?" Her tone was low, and her intent was clear. "You're delusional if you think I'm letting you anywhere near my house and my money. Let him go to college, you little slut. Set him free."

Our chests were so close I could hear her breaths. The room was warm, but I was cold. Nothing felt right. Nothing.

"He is free," I sneered, shaking my head. "He chose me."

"Then don't give him the option," she gritted, fury making the muscles on her face tic.

"Why? Because you said so?" Our faces were almost touching, too close for my liking, but I didn't back down. Our chests brushed, and I hated the scent of her Chanel No. 5 and expensive cosmetics in my nostrils.

"Because I have a lot of power in this town. Because what you're doing is wrong," she bit out, finishing on a whisper, "because no one can know this ever happened. Not to a family like the Followhills."

I was tempted to say she should remind herself of their reputation next time she jumped into bed with one of her staff, but that was Jaime's secret to tell, not mine. I would never out what he knew.

"Not scared of you or of getting kicked out of town," I retorted, only half doing it to push back at her. "Jaime was eighteen. This wasn't illegal."

"But it's still forbidden," she yelled, throwing her hands in the air. I turned and moved for the door. She jerked me by the arm, making me slam to a halt. "Your teaching career will be over, and I'll make certain the *La Belle* arson sticks to you."

Her hand wrapped around my elbow. "My deal is off the table the minute you step out of this office. I'll call the police, Melody, and we all know who they work for."

Yes. The Spencers, who would stop at nothing to cover their son's ass. Just like Principal Followhill.

"You do that." I shook her away, fake smile and bravado plastered on my face. "See how it turns out."

I pivoted again, bolting to the door, but Jaime's mom—*my boyfriend's mom*—yanked me back into her office and shut it with a bang I was sure it was audible to everyone in the hallway.

"Christ, what the hell is wrong with you? I'm giving you a way out. Just leave my son alone, and I'll take care of the *La Belle* mess."

"I don't care what you do about that boat," I hissed into her face. My lips were trembling and my nose stung. There was nothing I wanted more than to scream and tear her office apart. I had to stay collected for Jaime's sake and the future of my career outside of All Saints High. "It's not *my* mess. Jaime courted me. Hell, Jaime manipulated me. Maybe he does have a bit of his mom in him after all. But the bottom line is we're together, and there's nothing you can do about it."

Those were the last words I told her before I managed to free myself from her grasp and get the hell out of there.

And those words would bite me in the ass later that day.

Chapter Thirteen

"**F**UCK," JAIME MUTTERED, HIS ARM extended above my shoulder, propped on the wall I was leaning against. He ran his other hand through his hair, frustrated.

I nodded, trying to regulate my breaths. He didn't have time to be mad, and he knew it. Rubbing his face and shaking his head, his gaze moved between me and the school building. We were tucked behind the concession stand at the footfall field, near the student parking lot.

"What the fuck, man? You *followed* me?"

"Hey, you knew where I lived, worked out, what I eat for breakfast, and my insurance carrier, all before we even kissed." I arched an eyebrow, reminding him that we were as bad as each other. At least when it came to one another. "She's got my necklace, and Toby says it was me."

"Of course he does." Jaime jerked me to him, squeezing me into a painful hug. "He'd never rat us out. The ball-less little dick. Your necklace was convenient. If he knew what you meant to me, he would've found another sorry-ass to blame."

"Your mother doesn't make idle threats. She's got connections everywhere. And the Rowlands are powerful, too. I'm a no one."

"Not true. You're my someone." He brushed his knuckles against my temple.

"I'm not going to jail," I stressed.

He shook his head. "Over my dead body, Little Ballerina. Let me talk to my mom."

"I'm not sure that's a good idea."

"I'm not sure I fucking care."

He left me, heading to his mother's office. At first, I stayed rooted in place, watching his broad back disappear behind the double doors of the school building. My fingers travelled to my naked collarbone, looking for my anchor, but it wasn't there.

Jaime was my anchor now. I had no one to trust but him.

A few minutes after he left, I walked to the teacher's lot and waited by my car, chewing on my nails. I was supposed to teach a class but had been excused for the rest of the day. I hated waiting for the verdict, for Jaime to try and persuade his mom not to frame me for something we all knew I didn't do.

Ten minutes after he walked into her office, my cell phone buzzed.

"Join us," he commanded, in a tone I couldn't decode.

I did.

My knees wobbled and my breath sputtered as I walked the hallways of All Saints for what I had a feeling would be the last time. I knocked on Followhill's door and marched in.

"Come." Jaime patted a spot on the burgundy leather sofa beside him, his eyes hard on his mom. He was sitting in front of her, and it looked like her desk was the only thing keeping them from pouncing at each other. The air was thick with revulsion.

Jaime's expression was frustratingly blank. When I tried to read his mother's face, I didn't see love or compassion, either. Just disappointment…and urgency. Urgency to keep a legacy, to protect her family name. To keep the pride, money, and a lot of other tasteless shit in order.

My insides lurched, and for the first time, I realized I wasn't the only one who'd suffered destiny's wounds.

Just because Jaime didn't act like he'd been ripped to shreds didn't mean he was any happier than I was. No. We were both defective, chipped, and programmed to fight back. Sculpted by our fate. Scarred by who we were.

I was a dancer trapped in a teacher's life.

He was a free man imprisoned in his parents' ridiculous demands and great expectations.

I slouched next to Jaime, blinking away some of my shock. Fuck my life. Principal Miranda Followhill was the one in the wrong. But I did feel shame for caving into this affair with her son.

Shame over who I fell in love with.

Because that was the problem with society. It cared too much about *who* you fell in love with but never about the *why*. The why matters. The who is irrelevant (but the band was great, so there's that).

"We've reached an agreement." Mrs. Followhill's face tightened into a thin-lipped smile.

This didn't sound good. I nodded. Barely.

"And I think everyone shall benefit from this little arrangement."

Another beat of silence.

"Are you planning on announcing it at the LA Coliseum? Spit it out." I was no longer able to hide my true feelings for the woman.

Jaime snickered beside me, grabbing my hand and squeezing, his warmth seeping into me.

Mrs. Followhill scowled, unimpressed by my sass. "Jaime is going to move to Texas for college. In fact, he re-confirmed his attendance minutes ago on the phone with his dean. You will be let go after this school year. Your contract will not be renewed. You will not see each other anymore. In exchange, I will overlook the necklace found at the marina."

Her grin was victorious.

Yet all I saw was black.

My hand slid from Jaime's. Determined not to say anything, I fought the feeling of humiliation. He'd basically refused to fight for us, accepting her demand to go to Texas as he'd always planned. I simply shrugged. Whether he had shitty negotiation skills or he simply didn't care about me and was just using me didn't matter. His end game was the same. And guess who was the loser? Yup, *me*.

Jaime could have easily told his mother the truth. His mother protects him. From anything. I wasn't naïve enough to believe it was out of love. It was out of prestige and other meaningless things she cared about. Sure, she would give him hell, but she would also give him a way out.

He compromised me.

After he told me he wanted to protect me.

"Are you—have you spoken to the dean?" I jerked my head to look him in the eye. He sucked his cheeks in with a heavy sigh, nodding.

"Yeah. I'm moving to Austin."

"Sounds good to me."

"It does, huh?" Mrs. Followhill looked skeptical. Maybe even a little disappointed with my calmness. Her eyes glinted with ire, her lips thin and pressed together.

You can't win if I don't let you, I thought bitterly. *And I'm not. I'm not letting you see me break.*

"Yup. I mean, school's almost over. It was a nice fling." My lips curved into a smile, and I felt Jaime tensing beside me. I had a feeling there was a lot he wanted to explain. I wouldn't give him the chance though.

I hated him.

I hated *me*.

We deserved this heartache.

I felt his fingers trying to reconnect with mine and folded my arms over my chest, leaning back. I'd suffered enough whiplash from his mother. I was not going to be humiliated twice by getting dumped by her teenage son, listening to some "It's not you, it's me" bullshit.

"Guess it's time to say goodbye. I won't miss All Saints very much. And I definitely won't miss you, Mrs. Followhill. For a wealthy woman, your social skills are actually quite poor."

Translation: You're a bitch from hell, and I can't believe I actually thought your son would grow up to be any different. He obviously takes after you, even if he made me believe that he was anything but.

With that, I stood up. Jaime's gaze followed me, but I didn't risk looking at him. The confusion on his face was obvious, even if our eyes hadn't met. For the first time, I'd hurt a Followhill instead of having a Followhill hurt me. It made me feel lighter somehow, and that made me feel guilty.

Did I want Jaime to feel bad? *Why?*

"Melody." Jaime's voice was thick and dark. I shook my head.

"Let her leave, sweetheart," Principal Followhill instructed, resting her palm on his back.

He stood, pushing his chair back abruptly.

I needed to get out of there. "Yeah." I threw my bag over my shoulder, collecting my cell phone and keys. "We're done here."

I made my way out, leaving the boy-man who broke my heart and his bitchy mother behind me. He was moving to Texas. I shouldn't have been so disappointed. I pushed him in this direction. And his mom didn't leave us much choice. But I was hurt, so I'd stabbed him back with my words.

Jaime didn't follow me.

We'd both fucked up and had nothing to say to each other.

That day, I cried for all the years I hadn't cried. Buckets of tears. They were salty and sad and desperate.

They all tasted weird.

They all tasted like him.

Chapter Fourteen

JAIME DIDN'T COME TO OUR apartment that day. He didn't call. Not surprising, considering I'd reduced him to a short fling. After continuously pushing him away. After telling him he should move to Texas. After bitching about his best friend.

I wasn't a good girlfriend.

Nurturing wasn't my nature. I was sewn together with tattered patches of consuming ambition and shattered dreams. Up until now, I had been stupidly proud of that. Proud that I didn't let mundane things like love or a man consume me.

But now, when my heart hurt like it was butchered into minis-cule pieces, I realized what I was missing out on. Even the pain felt sweeter under the haze of love.

The next day, I showed up to teach Lit, and I was considering suicide by halfway into my third class of the day. The warning had been lifted by Jaime, and my students no longer played nice with me. They laughed, screamed, and talked back. Even more than before, it seemed. My last hour was the worst. Dean and Millie were silent, but Trent Rexroth went the extra mile and fingered Keeley, who sat next to him, under his desk, all while keeping a straight face and talking about the future of the Raiders with Vicious extra-loudly.

Asking Trent to put his hands where I could see them only drew more attention to him and the chick he was making out with, and I heard snickers when I turned my back to produce a book from my bag, probably because he shoved his tongue into her throat the minute he left my line of sight.

It was hell, and it was exactly where I deserved to be.

Jaime wasn't in class, even though it was the last time I would have taught him. It only confirmed what I already knew: Trent did what he did on purpose, and on Jaime's behalf.

They all hated me.

My heart sank in disappointment. I tried to concentrate on teaching, but my mind kept drifting to him.

I'd fucked up.

I didn't even give him the chance to explain after the meeting with his mom. Just naturally assumed he'd betrayed me. But it was Jaime. Jaime never betrayed anyone. He stood by those he cared about. Even by Vicious...

Vicious.

When the bell rang, I rose from my seat, piercing Jaime's BFF with my eyes.

"Baron." I signaled him to come closer.

He snorted but did as I asked. The classroom had already emptied, leaving just the two of us sizing each other up suspiciously.

"Where's Jaime?" I asked, rubbing my tired eyes. I didn't sleep much last night.

"The fuck do you care?" He tucked a cigarette between his lips, lighting it in class casually. "You keep tabs on all your *flings*?" he mumbled, the cigarette between his lips.

Someone was bitter.

"I need to talk to him," I said, ignoring the jab.

"Am I stopping you?"

"Tell me where he is."

He shrugged. "I'm not his goddamned secretary. Call him."

"He won't pick up," I cried in annoyance.

Vicious slid his thumb across his cheek with the hand that held his cigarette, deep in thought. "Yeah, he won't." His voice was chillingly flat. "He's at my house. Sulking like a little bitch. I'd invite you over to cheer him up, but I'm not sure if you wanna give him a lippy rant for saving your ass or a blow job for fucking up."

"I need to talk to him." The urgency in my voice scared me. The need to make this right was overwhelming. I just wanted us to work this out.

"I'm not him." Vicious's lifeless eyes held mine, sucking me in. "I don't do forgiveness, so if you hurt him again, the outcome will be devastating. To you."

Gulp. "I just want to fix this, Baron."

"My name is Vicious," he growled.

Goddammit. *This kid.*

"Let me see him. I promise, my intentions are good."

The HotHoles' brotherhood was almost touching, if it weren't for the fact that these boys had way too much power. Over me. Over this town. Over everyone.

Vicious tilted his head to the door, and I followed him to his brooding stone and brick mansion, my Ford stalking his Mercedes.

It was the longest journey I ever had to take, other than my flight back home from New York and Julliard.

But it was the shortest trip to insanity. My love was madness.

And I was ready to fight for it.

Chapter Fifteen

H E WAS IN THE POOL. In the goddamn fucking pool. Doing laps. His long, lean sculpted body shooting like an arrow from one end to the other. I stood over the edge, not sure if I wanted to jump his bones, apologize, or yell at him. When he raised his head from the azure waterline, dark blond locks raining water drops over his perfect face, my thighs clenched.

"You look heartbroken," I assessed sarcastically.

He rested his arms on the tiles and flashed me his straight teeth. But this wasn't a smile, it was a warning. "And you look like an animal out of its natural habitat. Missed me that much, Ms. G?"

"You didn't come to school today." My voice was grave.

"So? School year is practically over, and it's not like you give a shit. I'm just a fling, remember? Your words."

Touché.

When I arrived here, I wasn't above begging. But now that I was in front of him, at Vicious's house, an overwhelming need to protect myself took over again. I couldn't ask him what his game was yesterday when we were at his mother's office.

"So, you're all packed for Texas?" I changed the subject. *He's moving away to college,* I reminded myself. *This is over.*

He laughed, pushing himself upward and rising from the pool. His sculpted body shone under the sun, making him look like a Calvin Klein ad. He stood next to me, so close the scent of chlorine wafted into my nostrils.

"Not yet." He took a step in my direction. I stumbled back. He took another step closer, ignoring me.

"I need to buy another suitcase." His hand disappeared inside my curls. This time I leaned into his touch. *Such a loser. Already a goner again.*

"I thought men traveled light." I swallowed.

"We do, but I'm sure you'll be taking all kinds of girly shit with you when you move in with me."

Dumbfounded, I narrowed my eyes at him, fighting a grin.

"Jaime," I warned. From what, I wasn't sure. I didn't want it to be a prank. I realized as soon as he said the words that I wanted exactly what he'd just said. A lot. A new beginning. Away from All Saints High. With him.

It didn't make sense. It was wrong. It was going to lift a shit-ton of eyebrows. A college kid moving to another state with his twenty-six-year-old teacher? It had disaster written all over it. But I wanted this disaster. I wanted to bathe in it and love it and *live* it. To make this disaster my chaotic reality.

"Mel," he answered, smiling. "Truth or dare?"

"Truth." I bit my lower lip, peeking at him from under my lashes. If Vicious saw this, he would have probably puked.

My breaths were coming in shallow pants. My heart was in my throat. I hadn't felt this alive since the last time I was on stage. I was going to say it, and fuck the world and what it'd think about me.

I placed my hands on top of his, still nestled in my hair, holding me still. "The truth is…I love you."

There was a hint of a satisfied smile, but it was quick. Like I was still in trouble. I felt like the scolded student.

He nodded, his wet hair dripping on my face as he hooked an arm around my neck and jerked me into his face. "See? Was that so hard? Still in one piece, aren't you, baby girl?" He raised an eyebrow at me in a smart-ass expression, and it was sexy as fuck. "I love you, too, Mel. Fucking crazy about you, actually. Now pack up." He bit my lip playfully, smacking my ass at the exact same time.

"Excuse me?" I laughed. "What? Where? How? When? School's not even over yet."

There were four more days left of school. And I still hadn't said yes to moving to a whole other state with him.

"Yeah, but you have a job interview at a ballet academy in Austin tomorrow. Don't wanna be late, yeah? Bad first impression and all."

Jaime knew. He knew I pocketed this dream in the back of my jeans, but still danced every day in front of the mirror. That I carried it in my heart like a little souvenir, and that I wanted the memory to become something real, now more than ever.

Just then, a horn honked in the distance, and I heard Vicious grit behind his fancy Mercedes steering wheel. "Tell her to move her ass, or I'm sending you both to the airport in a cab."

These high school kids.

They had planned it all along.

They outsmarted Mrs. Followhill and me.

I laughed, collapsing into my boyfriend's arms. "Damn you."

Epilogue

Two years later…

"YOU FORGOT THE MILK."

"You forgot your underwear."

I frown, pushing down my black tights. "I'm wearing underwear."

"Exactly." Jaime pushes me to bed in one effortless movement.

I collapse onto our flimsy mattress. He follows, crushing on top of me, covering my face and neck with wet, hot kisses. Breathless giggles escape my mouth while his fingers push my tights away.

"I'll buy some on my way back from my shift," Jaime growls into my ribcage.

My shirt is already tossed aside, and he is sucking on my nipple so hard my skull prickles in pleasure. I sigh and rake my fingers through his tousled blond hair. He's been taking shifts at a local Starbucks after class. His parents cut him off after we announced we were moving in together. Tough luck. With my work at the ballet academy, his school and Starbucks job, and everything else on our plate, we have very little time to give two shits about what other people think or say.

"Can you get some fruit as well? We're out of bananas."

"There's one banana you can eat whenever you want, and it's right here." He takes my hand, guiding it to his cock.

I roll my eyes. Yup, still a typical twenty-year-old. I'm twenty-eight now, and you'd think I'd be obsessing over marriage and babies. But I'm not. All I think about is him. How it worked out so fabulously. It's our beautiful chaos, and we wouldn't have it any other way.

"I might take a bite later," I tease.

He winces. "Fine, I'll get you your stupid fruit, woman."

His tongue travels down from my stomach to my now bare pussy, and he halts, his nose rubbing circles against my clit. "Oh, I think you have something here. Like a scratch or a spot or something." His hand dives between my legs, and when it rises back up, there's a small black velvet box in his hand.

I stop breathing altogether.

He licks his lips, offering a lazy smile. "I probably should warn you, it's not an engagement ring. I'm waiting to turn twenty-one so the trust fund my grandparents have under my name will kick in. I'll be richer and Starbucks-free. You deserve something incredible. But in the meantime, here's something to make you remember your high school fling from two years ago."

With shaky fingers, I open the velvet box and inside rests a necklace. With a charm. A golden anchor. This anchor symbolizing so many things.

The burnt yacht that ripped us apart.

The necklace that brought us back together.

The missing piece I left behind.

My eyes glide up, piercing him with uncontained love. I'm so in love. So completely out-of-my-mind crazy about this boy who grew up to be a man and has given up so many things to be with me. College party life. Football. Things that were his very essence of being two years ago.

111

"Help me?" I motion with the necklace between my fingers.

He grunts at my request for him to unglue his tongue from my inner thigh, but rises to face me. Taking the necklace from my hand, he brushes my hair aside.

"Truth or dare?" he asks out of nowhere.

"Truth. Brave people always choose the truth." I grin.

"Is it true that you'll always be mine?" He lowers his mouth to my ear, his warm breath tickling my skin.

"It's a truth. And sometimes, when you piss me off, it's a dare. But it's my life, and you're a part of it. Always and forever," I say.

"Always and forever," he repeats, and I hold on to my anchor, squeezing it—and my real-life anchor—hard.

The angst. The fear. The part where I let myself go and fall in love with who should've been the wrong person but who turned out to be right, so right…it's all behind us now.

In the end, it was worth it. Every small piece of who made us who we are today.

Stronger.

Happier.

Wholer.

Six Years Later…

Jaime

"Why the anchor?"

I probably should have asked that eight years ago, when we first met, but I just couldn't bring myself to it. I considered it pillow talk, and I was feeling pretty fucking frightened as it was about stalking my Lit teacher.

I'm watching my wife, Melody Followhill, intently, as she rests

112

her feet on top of the coffee table while leaning back on our new couch. The sofa and the table are the only pieces of furniture in our new Kensington apartment—or 'flat', as they call it here in London. I said I'd take her to Europe, and I did. The fact I knocked her up here is just a bonus.

You're welcome, Mel.

"Why the anchor?" she parrots me, grinning as she rubs her thirty-six-week belly, staring at it lovingly as if she can already see our newborn daughter. "Because sometimes, it's nice to feel like there's someone who can save you."

"Who gave you that necklace?" I shoot. The urgency of my questions startles me. I've lasted eight years without asking her that, and suddenly, that's all I want to know about. Melody leans into me, placing her head on my chest. I brush her brown hair from her face and kiss her temple. When she talks, warmth fills my chest.

"I bought it for myself. I was at JFK airport, just about to board the plane back to California after breaking my leg. I wanted something to believe in. More like – *someone* to believe in. I had no one. My parents were supportive and sad for me, but they didn't understand. Not really. My friends were scattered all around the country, chasing their own college dreams, creating new, sweet memories. And there I was. Alone. I needed someone. I saw this necklace at a store. I don't even remember the name. They sold hoodies saying "I Love New York" for ridiculous prices. It cost me a lot, but I remember thinking to myself – I need this. I'm going to get this."

I look down, staring at her eyes, and I'm amazed. Amazed that this woman is mine. After all we've been through—and maybe precisely because of that.

She is funny and strong. So fucking talented, sarcastic and smart. But at the same time, she is real. And vulnerable. And mine. God, damn, so fucking mine.

"You don't need it anymore." I finger the anchor necklace I

gave her when I was in college. "You have me."

"I need both," she smiles, kissing my pecs through my shirt.

She is wrong.

She doesn't need anybody.

She can conquer the world, in her sensible shoes and knee-length dresses, not giving a damn about what anyone thinks.

I take her hand, kiss her palm and guide it to my raging erection. I'm always hard for this woman. Always.

"You mean the three of us?" I grin into her lips, and she clutches my jeans, a little too hard for my liking.

"You know what I need?" she asks, and for some reason, there's sweat coating her beautiful forehead. I cock one eyebrow.

"I need you to drive me to the hospital. My water just broke."

"I knew you were hard for me." I lick her neck, and she punches my arm. Hard.

"Jaime!"

"Okay, okay, I'll grab your bag."

Fifteen hours later, Melody and I welcome our first daughter, Daria Sophia Followhill. My parents are boarding a plane from San Diego to see her. They're excited. Mel's parents are coming, too, at the end of the month.

My father still doesn't know about mom and coach Rowland. I never told him. There was never much point.

He doesn't love her, and she doesn't love him.

They have so much money. So many means. And here I am, with a wife and a new baby, still cut-off from their fortune because of the choices I took.

And I'm happy, because I don't need money. I have my girls, and that's enough.

It. Is. Everything.

The End

The Sinners of Saint is a five-book series of interconnected standalones. Make sure you read the rest of the book in the series:

Vicious (Sinners of Saint #1)

Ruckus (Sinners of Saint #2)

Scandalous (Sinners of Saint #3)

Bane (Sinners of Saint #4)

Can't get enough of the HotHoles? See what their kids are up to in the all-new, New Adult series All Saints High. They are ALL standalones and can be read out of order, just like the Sinners of Saint:

Pretty Reckless (All Saints High #1)

Broken Knight (All Saints High #2)

Angry God (All Saints High #3)

Acknowledgements

A list of people who I am forever grateful for and love more than life itself:

Sunny Borek
Kristina Lindsey
Karen Dale Harris
Ellie McLove
Stacey Blake
Letitia Hasser
Brittany Hale
Sabrina Shalalashvilli
Becca Zsurkan
Avivit Egev
Sher Mason
Sheena Taylor
Lin Tahel Cohen
Amy Halter
Paige Jennifer
Ilor Tsabar
Vanessa Serrano
Erika Budd Panfile
Galit Hadar Shmariyaho
Jessica Meade
Kristen Reads
Karin Boukzam
Ella Fox
Ava Harrison
Tanaka Kangara

Julia E. Lis
Bernadett Lankovitz
Kerissa Blake
And Tamar Hazan.

I would also like to take this opportunity to thank my Sassy Sparrows group, and to my family, for being thoughtful and understanding. Truly, I couldn't be more grateful.

To the wonderful bloggers who continue sharing and supporting my work. I cherish you and your amazing contribution to the indie community. And, as always, to you, readers, for taking a chance on me.

Thank you, thank you, thank you (I find my own acknowledgements speech quite underwhelming, but it's not as bad as Tom Hiddleton's Golden Globes speech, so there's that),
Love you all, more than you can ever imagine,

L.J.
xoxo

Books by

L.J. SHEN

Standalones:

Tyed

Sparrow

Blood to Dust

Midnight Blue

Dirty Headlines

The Kiss Thief

Sinners of Saints (all interconnected standalones):

Vicious (Sinners of Saint #1)

Defy (Sinners of Saint #0.5 – Novella)

Ruckus (Sinners of Saint #2)

Scandalous (Sinners of Saint #3)

Bane (Sinners of Saint #4)

All Saints High:

Pretty Reckless (All Saints High #1)

Broken Knight (All Saints High #2)

Angry God (All Saints High #3)

KEEP IN TOUCH

Join L.J. Shen's Newsletter: http://eepurl.com/b8pSuP

Join L.J. Shen's Reading Group: goo.gl/5D2kTf

Like her Facebook Page: goo.gl/xlbtkX

Stalk Her Instagram (warning: mainly pictures of sushi):

goo.gl/9rllfd

And Don't Forget Twitter: goo.gl/ox9pkV

VICIOUS SNEAK PEEK

Before you leave: here is a sneak peek to *Vicious* (Sinners of Saint #1). *Vicious* is now available, so make sure to grab it if you like the first chapter!

Chapter One

Emilia

MY GRANDMAMA ONCE TOLD ME that love and hate are the same feelings experienced under different circumstances. The passion is the same. The pain is the same. That weird thing that bubbles in your chest? Same. I didn't believe her until I met Baron Spencer and he became my nightmare.

Then my nightmare became my reality.

I thought I'd escaped him. I was even stupid enough to think he'd forgotten I ever existed.

But when he came back, he hit harder than I ever thought possible.

And just like a domino—I fell.

Ten Years Ago

I'd only been inside the mansion once before, when my family first came to Todos Santos. That was two months ago. That day, I stood rooted in place on the same ironwood flooring that never creaked.

That first time, Mama had elbowed my ribs. "You know this is the toughest floor in the world?"

She failed to mention it belonged to the man with the toughest heart in the world.

I couldn't for the life of me understand why people with so much money would spend it on such a depressing house. Ten bedrooms. Thirteen bathrooms. An indoor gym and a dramatic staircase. The best amenities money could buy...and except for the tennis court and sixty-five-foot pool, they were all in black.

Black choked out every pleasant feeling you might possibly have as soon as you walked through the big iron-studded doors. The interior designer must've been a medieval vampire, judging from the cold, lifeless colors and the giant iron chandeliers hanging from the ceilings. Even the floor was so dark that it looked like I was hovering over an abyss, a fraction of a second from falling into nothingness.

A ten-bedroom house, three people living in it—two of them barely ever there—and the Spencers had decided to house my family in the servants' apartment near the garage. It was bigger than our clapboard rental in Richmond, Virginia, but until that moment, it had still rubbed me the wrong way.

Not anymore.

Everything about the Spencer mansion was designed to intimidate. Rich and wealthy, yet poor in so many ways. *These are not happy people,* I thought.

I stared at my shoes—the tattered white Vans I doodled colorful flowers on to hide the fact that they were knock-offs—and swallowed, feeling insignificant even before *he* had belittled me. Before I even knew *him*.

"I wonder where he is?" Mama whispered.

As we stood in the hallway, I shivered at the echo that bounced off the bare walls. She wanted to ask if we could get paid two days early because we needed to buy medicine for my younger sister, Rosie.

"I hear something coming from that room." She pointed to a door on the opposite side of the vaulted foyer. "You go knock. I'll go back to the kitchen to wait."

"*Me?* Why me?"

"Because," she said, pinning me with a stare that stabbed at my conscience, "Rosie's sick, and his parents are out of town. You're his age. He'll listen to you."

I did as I was told—not for Mama, for Rosie—without understanding the consequences. The next few minutes cost me my whole senior year and were the reason why I was ripped from my family at the age of eighteen.

Vicious thought I knew his secret.

I didn't.

He thought I'd found out what he was arguing about in that room that day.

I had no clue.

All I remember was trudging toward the threshold of another dark door, my fist hovering inches from it before I heard the deep rasp of an old man.

"You know the drill, Baron."

A man. A smoker, probably.

"My sister told me you're giving her trouble again." The man slurred his words before raising his voice and slapping his palm against a hard surface. "I've had enough of you disrespecting her."

"Fuck you." I heard the composed voice of a younger man. He sounded…amused? "And fuck her too. Wait, is that why you're here, Daryl? You want a piece of your sister too? The good news is that she's open for business, if you have the buck to pay."

"Look at the mouth on you, you little cunt." *Slap.* "Your mother would've been proud."

Silence, and then, "Say another word about my mother, and I'll give you a real reason to get those dental implants you were talking about with my dad." The younger man's voice dripped venom, which made me think he might not be as young as Mama thought.

"Stay away," the younger voice warned. "I can beat the shit out of you, now. As a matter of fact, I'm pretty tempted to do so. All. The fucking. Time. I'm done with your shit."

"And what the hell makes you think you have a choice?" The older man chuckled darkly.

I felt his voice in my bones, like poison eating at my skeleton.

"Haven't you heard?" the younger man gritted out. "I like to fight. I like the pain. Maybe because it makes it so much easier for me to come to terms with the fact that I'm going to kill you one day. And I will, Daryl. One day, I will kill you."

I gasped, too stunned to move. I heard a loud smack, then someone tumbling down, dragging some items with him as he fell to the floor.

I was about to run—this conversation obviously wasn't meant for me to hear—but he caught me off guard. Before I knew what was happening, the door swung open and I came face to face with a boy around my age. I say *a boy,* but there was nothing boyish about him.

The older man stood behind him, panting hard, hunched with his hands flat against a desk. Books were scattered around his feet, and his lip was cut and bleeding.

The room was a library. Soaring floor-to-ceiling, walnut shelves full of hardbacks lined the walls. I felt a pang in my chest because I somehow knew there wasn't any way I'd ever be allowed in there again.

"What the fuck?" the teenage boy seethed. His eyes narrowed. They felt like the sight of a rifle aimed at me.

Seventeen? Eighteen? The fact that we were about the same age somehow made everything about the situation worse. I ducked my head, my cheeks flaming with enough heat to burn down the whole house.

"Have you been listening?" His jaw twitched.

I frantically shook my head *no*, but that was a lie. I'd always been a terrible liar.

"I didn't hear a thing, I swear." I choked on my words. "My mama works here. I was looking for her." Another lie.

I'd never been a scaredy-cat. I was always the brave one. But I didn't feel so brave at that moment. After all, I wasn't supposed to be there, in his house, and I definitely wasn't supposed to be listening to their argument.

The young man took a step closer, and I took a step back. His eyes were dead, but his lips were red, full, and very much alive. *This guy is going to break my heart if I let him.* The voice came from somewhere inside my head, and the thought stunned me because it made no sense at all. I'd never fallen in love before, and I was too anxious to even register his eye color or hairstyle, let alone the notion of ever having any feelings for the guy.

"What's your name?" he demanded. He smelled delicious—a masculine spice of boy-man, sweet sweat, sour hormones, and the faint trace of clean laundry, one of my mama's many chores.

"Emilia." I cleared my throat and extended my arm. "My friends call me Millie. Y'all can too."

His expression revealed zero emotion. "You're fucking done, *Emilia*." He drawled my name, mocking my Southern accent and not even acknowledging my hand with a glance.

I withdrew it quickly, embarrassment flaming my cheeks again.

"Wrong fucking place and wrong fucking time. Next time I find you anywhere inside my house, bring a body bag because you won't be leaving alive." He thundered past me, his muscular arm brushing my shoulder.

I choked on my breath. My gaze bolted to the older man, and our eyes locked. He shook his head and grinned in a way that made me want to fold into myself and disappear. Blood dripped from his lip onto his leather boot—black like his worn MC jacket. What was he doing in a place like this, anyway? He just stared at me, making no move to clean up the blood.

I turned around and ran, feeling the bile burning in my throat, threatening to spill over.

Needless to say, Rosie had to make do without her medicine that week and my parents were paid not a minute earlier than when they were scheduled to.

That was two months ago.

Today, when I walked through the kitchen and climbed the stairs, I had no choice.

I knocked on Vicious's bedroom door. His room was on the second floor at the end of the wide curved hallway, the door facing the floating stone staircase of the cave-like mansion.

I'd never been near Vicious's room, and I wished I could keep it that way. Unfortunately, my calculus book had been stolen. Whoever broke into my locker had wiped it clean of my stuff and left garbage inside. Empty soda cans, cleaning supplies, and condom wrappers spilled out the minute I opened the locker door.

Just another not-so-clever, yet effective, way for the students at All Saints High to remind me that I was nothing but the cheap help around here. By that point, I was so used to it I barely reddened at all. When all eyes in the hallway darted to me, snickers and chuckles rising out of every throat, I tilted my chin up and marched straight to my next class.

All Saints High was a school full of spoiled, over-privileged sinners. A school where if you failed to dress or act a certain way, you didn't belong. Rosie blended in better than I did, thank the Lord. But with a Southern drawl, off-beat style, and one of the most popular guys at school—that being Vicious Spencer—hating my guts, I didn't fit in.

What made it worse was that I didn't *want* to fit in. These kids didn't impress me. They weren't kind or welcoming or even very smart. They didn't possess any of the qualities I looked for in friends.

But I needed my textbook badly if I ever wanted to escape this place.

I knocked three times on the mahogany door of Vicious's bedroom. Rolling my lower lip between my fingers, I tried to suck in as much oxygen as I could, but it did nothing to calm the throbbing pulse in my neck.

Please don't be there...

Please don't be an ass...

Please...

A soft noise seeped from the crack under the door, and my body tensed.

Giggling.

Vicious never giggled. Heck, he hardly ever chuckled. Even his smiles were few and far between. No. The sound was undoubtedly female.

I heard him whisper in his raspy tone something inaudible that made her moan. My ears seared, and I anxiously rubbed my hands on the yellow cut-off denim shorts covering my thighs. Out of all the scenarios I could have imagined, this was by far the worst.

Him.

With another girl.

Who I hated before I even knew her name.

It didn't make any sense, yet I felt ridiculously angry.

But he was clearly there, and I was a girl on a mission.

"Vicious?" I called out, trying to steady my voice. I straightened my spine, even though he couldn't see me. "It's Millie. Sorry to interrupt, y'all. I just wanted to borrow your calc book. Mine's lost, and I really need to get ready for that exam we have tomorrow."

God forbid you ever study for our exam yourself, I breathed silently.

He didn't answer, but I heard a sharp intake of breath—*the girl*—and the rustle of fabric and the noise of a zipper rolling. Down, I had no doubt.

I squeezed my eyes shut and pressed my forehead against the cool wood of his door.

Bite the bullet. Swallow your pride. This wouldn't matter in a few years. Vicious and his stupid antics would be a distant memory, the snooty town of Todos Santos just a dust-covered part of my past.

My parents had jumped at the chance when Josephine Spencer offered them a job. They'd dragged us across the country to California because the health care was better and we didn't even need to pay rent. Mama was the Spencers' cook/housekeeper, and Daddy was part gardener and handyman. The previous live-in couple had quit, and it was no wonder. Pretty sure my parents weren't so keen on the job either. But opportunities like these were rare, and Josephine Spencer's mama was friends with my great-aunt, which is how they'd gotten the job.

I was planning on getting out of here soon. As soon as I got accepted to the first out-of-state college I'd applied to, to be exact. In order to do so, though, I needed a scholarship.

For a scholarship, I needed kick-ass grades.

And for kick-ass grades, I needed this textbook.

"Vicious," I ground out his stupid nickname. I knew he hated his real name, and for reasons beyond my grasp, I didn't want to upset him. "I'll grab the book and copy the formulas I need real quick. I won't borrow it long. Please." I gulped down the ball of frustration twisting in my throat. It was bad enough I'd had my stuff stolen—*again*—without having to ask Vicious for favors.

The giggling escalated. The high, screechy pitch sawed through my ears. My fingers tingled to push the door open and launch at him with my fists.

I heard his groan of pleasure and knew it had nothing to do with the girl he was with. He loved taunting me. Ever since our first encounter outside of his library two months ago, he'd been hell-bent on reminding me that I wasn't good enough.

Not good enough for his mansion.

Not good enough for his school.

Not good enough for *his town*.

Worst part? It wasn't a figure of speech. It really *was* his town. Baron Spencer Jr.—dubbed Vicious for his cold, ruthless behavior—was the heir to one of the biggest family-owned fortunes in California. The Spencers owned a pipeline company, half of downtown Todos Santos—including the mall—and three corporate office parks. Vicious had enough money to take care of the next ten generations of his family.

But I didn't.

My parents were servants. We had to work for every penny. I didn't expect him to understand. Trust-fund kids never did. But I presumed he'd at least pretend, like the rest of them.

Education mattered to me, and at that moment, I felt robbed of it.

Because rich people had stolen my books.

Because this particular rich kid wouldn't even open the door to his room so I could borrow his textbook real quick.

"Vicious!" My frustration got the better of me, and I slammed my palm flat against his door. Ignoring the throb it sent up my wrist, I continued, exasperated. "C'mon!"

I was close to turning around and walking away. Even if it meant I had to take my bike and ride all the way across town to borrow Sydney's books. Sydney was my only friend at All Saints

High, and the one person I liked in class.

But then I heard Vicious chuckling, and I knew the joke was on me. "I love to see you crawl. Beg for it, baby, and I'll give it to you," he said.

Not to the girl in his room.

To me.

I lost it. Even though I knew it was wrong. That he was winning.

I thrust the door open and barged into his room, strangling the handle with my fist, my knuckles white and burning.

My eyes darted to his king-sized bed, barely stopping to take in the gorgeous mural above it—four white horses galloping into the darkness—or the elegant dark furniture. His bed looked like a throne, sitting in the middle of the room, big and high and draped in soft black satin. He was perched on the edge of his mattress, a girl who was in my PE class in his lap. Her name was Georgia and her grandparents owned half the vineyards upstate in Carmel Valley. Georgia's long blonde hair veiled one of his broad shoulders and her Caribbean tan looked perfect and smooth against Vicious's pale complexion.

His dark blue eyes—so dark they were almost black—locked on mine as he continued to kiss her ravenously—his tongue making several appearances—like she was made of cotton candy. I needed to look away, but couldn't. I was trapped in his gaze, completely immobilized from the eyes down, so I arched an eyebrow, showing him that I didn't care.

Only I did. I cared a lot.

I cared so much, in fact, that I continued to stare at them shamelessly. At his hollowed cheeks as he inserted his tongue deep into her mouth, his burning, taunting glare never leaving mine, gauging me for a reaction. I felt my body buzzing in an unfamiliar way, falling under his spell. A sweet, pungent fog. It was sexual, unwelcome, yet completely inescapable. I wanted to break free, but for the life of me, I couldn't.

My grip on the door handle tightened, and I swallowed, my eyes dropping to his hand as he grabbed her waist and squeezed playfully. I squeezed my own waist through the fabric of my yellow-and-white sunflower top.

What the hell was wrong with me? Watching him kiss another girl was unbearable, but also weirdly fascinating.

I wanted to see it.

I didn't want to see it.

Either way, I couldn't *unsee* it.

Admitting defeat, I blinked, shifting my gaze to a black Raiders cap hung over the headrest of his desk chair.

"Your textbook, Vicious. I need it," I repeated. "I'm not leaving your room without it."

"Get the fuck out, Help," he said into Georgia's giggling mouth.

A thorn twisted in my heart, jealousy filling my chest. I couldn't wrap my head around this physical reaction. The pain. The shame. The *lust*. I hated Vicious. He was hard, heartless, and hateful. I'd heard his mother had died when he was nine, but he was eighteen now and had a nice stepmother who let him do whatever he wanted. Josephine seemed sweet and caring.

He had no reason to be so cruel, yet he was to everyone. Especially to me.

"Nope." Inside, rage pounded through me, but outside, I remained unaffected. "*Calc. Textbook.*" I spoke slowly, treating him like the idiot he thought I was. "Just tell me where it is. I'll leave it at your door when I'm done. Easiest way to get rid of me and get back to your...activities."

Georgia, who was fiddling with his zipper, her white sheath dress already unzipped from behind, growled, pushing away from his chest momentarily and rolling her eyes.

She squeezed her lips into a disapproving pout. "Really? Mindy?"—My name was Millie and she knew it—"Can't you find anything better to do with your time? He's a little out of your league, don't you think?"

Vicious took a moment to examine me, a cocky smirk plastered on his face. He was so damn handsome. Unfortunately. Black hair, shiny and trimmed fashionably, buzzed at the sides and longer on top. Indigo eyes, bottomless in their depth, sparkling and hardened. By what, I didn't know. Skin so pale he looked like a stunning ghost.

As a painter, I often spent time admiring Vicious's form. The angles of his face and sharp bone structure. All smooth edges. Defined and clear-cut. He was made to be painted. A masterpiece of nature.

Georgia knew it too. I'd heard her not too long ago talking about him in the locker room after PE. Her friend had said, "Beautiful guy."

"Dude, but *ugly* personality," Georgia was quick to add. A moment of silence passed before they'd both snorted out a laugh.

"Who cares?" Georgia's friend had concluded. "I'd still do him."

The worst part was I couldn't blame them.

He was both a baller and filthy rich—a popular guy who dressed and talked the right way. A perfect All Saints hero. He drove the right kind of car—Mercedes—and possessed that mystifying aura of a true alpha. He always had the room. Even when he was completely silent.

Feigning boredom, I crossed my arms and leaned one hip on his doorframe. I stared out his window, knowing tears would appear in my eyes if I looked directly at him or Georgia.

"His *league*?" I mocked. "I'm not even playing the same game. I don't play dirty."

"You will, once I push you far enough," Vicious snapped, his tone flat and humorless. It felt like he clawed my guts out and threw them on his pristine ironwood floor.

I blinked slowly, trying to look blasé. "Textbook?" I asked for the two-hundredth time.

He must've concluded he'd tortured me enough for one day. He cocked his head sideways to a backpack sitting under his desk. The window above it overlooked the servants' apartment where I lived, allowing him a perfect view directly into my room. So far, I'd caught him staring at me twice through the window, and I always wondered why.

Why, why, why?

He hated me so much. The intensity of his glare burned my face every time he looked at me, which wasn't as often as I'd like him to. But being the sensible girl that I was, I never allowed myself to dwell on it.

I marched to the Givenchy rubber-coated backpack he took to school every day and blew out air as I flipped it open, rummaging noisily through his things. I was glad my back was to them, and I tried to block out the moans and sucking noises.

The second my hand touched the familiar white-and-blue calc book, I stilled. I stared at the cherry blossom I'd doodled on the spine. Rage tingled up my spine, coursing through my veins, making my fists clench and unclench. Blood whooshed in my ears, and my breathing quickened.

He broke into my friggin' locker.

With shaking fingers, I pulled the book out of Vicious's backpack. "You stole my textbook?" I turned to face him, every muscle in my face tense.

This was an escalation. Blunt aggression. Vicious always taunted me, but he'd never humiliated me like this before. He'd stolen my things and stuffed my locker full of condoms and used toilet paper, for Christ's sake.

Our eyes met and tangled. He pushed Georgia off his lap, like she was an eager puppy he was done playing with, and stood up. I took a step forward. We were nose to nose now.

"Why are you doing this to me?" I hissed out, searching his blank, stony face.

"Because I can," he offered with a smirk to hide all the pain in his eyes.

What's eating you, Baron Spencer?

"Because it's fun?" he added, chuckling while throwing Georgia's jacket at her. Without a glance her way, he motioned for her to leave.

She was clearly nothing more than a prop. A means to an end. He'd wanted to hurt me.

And he succeeded.

I shouldn't care about why he acted this way. It made no difference at all. The bottom line was I hated him. I hated him so much it made me sick to my stomach that I loved the way he looked, on and off the field. Hated my shallowness, my foolishness, at loving the way his square, hard jaw ticked when he fought a smile. I hated that I loved the smart, witty things that came out of his mouth when he spoke in class. Hated that he was a cynical realist while I was a hopeless idealist, and still, I loved every thought he uttered aloud. And I hated that once a week, every week, my heart did crazy things in my chest because I suspected he might be *him*.

I hated him, and it was clear that he hated me back.

I hated him, but I hated Georgia more because she was the one he'd kissed.

Knowing full well I couldn't fight him—my parents worked here—I bit my tongue and stormed toward the door. I only made it to the threshold before his callused hand wrapped around my elbow, spinning me in place and throwing my body into his steel chest. I swallowed back a whimper.

"Fight me, Help," he snarled into my face, his nostrils flaring like a wild beast. His lips were close, so close. Still swollen from kissing another girl, red against his fair skin. "For once in your life, stand your fucking ground."

I shook out of his touch, clutching my textbook to my chest like it was my shield. I rushed out of his room and didn't stop to take a breath until I reached the servants' apartment. Swinging the door open, I bolted to my room and locked the door, plopping down on the bed with a heavy sigh.

I didn't cry. He didn't deserve my tears. But I was angry, upset and yes, a little broken.

In the distance, I heard music blasting from his room, getting louder by the second as he turned the volume up to the max. It took me a few beats to recognize the song. "Stop Crying Your Eyes Out" by Oasis.

A few minutes later, I heard Georgia's red automatic Camaro—the one Vicious constantly made fun of because, *Who the fuck buys an automatic Camaro?*—gun down the tree-lined driveway of the estate. She sounded angry too.

Vicious was vicious. It was too bad that my hate for him was dipped in a thin shell of something that felt like love. But I promised myself I'd crack it, break it, and unleash pure hatred in its place before he got to me. *He*, I promised myself, *will never break me.*

Chapter Two

VICIOUS

Ten Years Ago

IT WAS THE SAME OLD shit, different weekend, at my house. I was throwing another balls-out party and didn't even bother to leave the media/gaming room to hang out with the assholes I'd invited.

I knew what kind of chaos was teeming outside the room. The snickering and screaming girls in the kidney-shaped pool at the back of the house. The gurgles of the artificial waterfalls pouring out of the Greek arches into the water and the slap of rubber, inflated mattresses against bare, wet skin. The groans of couples fucking in nearby rooms. The mean-ass gossip of cliques crashing on the plush loveseats and sofas downstairs.

I heard music—Limp Bizkit—and who the fuck had the balls to play *Lame* Bizkit at my party?

I could've heard all the rest too if I wanted to, but I didn't *listen*. Sprawled out on my Wing Lounge chair in front of the TV, thighs open wide, I smoked a blunt and watched some anime Japanese porno.

There was a beer to my right, but I didn't touch it.

There was a chick on her knees below my seat, on the carpet, massaging my thighs, but I didn't touch her either.

"Vicious," she purred, inching closer to my groin. She slowly climbed up, straddling my lap.

A tan nameless brunette in a come-fuck-me dress. She looked like an Alicia or Lucia, maybe. Tried to get onto the cheerleading squad last spring. Failed. My guess was this party was her first taste of popularity. Hooking up with me, or anyone else in this room, was her shortcut to celebrity status at school.

For that reason alone, she was of no interest to me.

"Your media room is rad. Think we can go somewhere quieter, though?"

I tapped the head of my blunt, the ash falling to an ashtray on the arm of my chair like a flake of dirty snow. My jaw twitched. "No."

"But I like you."

Bullshit. Nobody liked me, and for good reason.

"I don't do relationships," I said on auto-pilot.

"Like, d'uh. I know that, silly. No harm in having some fun, though." She snorted, an unattractive laugh that made me hate her for trying so hard.

Self-respect went a long way in my book.

My eyes narrowed as I mulled over her offer. Sure, I could let her suck my dick, but I knew better than to believe her indifferent act. They all wanted something more.

"You should get out of here," I said, for the first and last time. I wasn't her dad. It wasn't my responsibility to warn her about guys like me.

She pouted, linking her arms behind my neck and scooting up my thigh. Her exposed cleavage pressed against my chest and her eyes burned with determination. "I'm not leaving here without one of you HotHoles."

I arched one eyebrow, exhaling smoke through my nose, my eyes hooded with boredom. "Then you better try Trent or Dean, 'cause I ain't fucking you tonight, sweetheart."

Alicia-Lucia pulled away, finally getting the hint. She sashayed to the bar with a fake smile, that crumpled with every step she took in those high heels, and fixed herself a bullshit cocktail without checking what liquor she poured into the tall glass. Her eyes were shiny as she scanned the room, trying to figure out which one of my friends—we were the Four HotHoles of All Saints High—was willing to be her ticket to popularity.

Trent was slouched on the couch to my right, half-sitting, half-lying as a random chick grinding on his cock, straddling him with her shirt pulled down to her waist and her bare tits bouncing almost comically. He put the beer bottle to his mouth and dicked around on his phone, jaded. Dean and Jaime sat on a loveseat on the other side, arguing about next week's football game. Neither of them had touched the girls we'd summoned into the room.

Jaime, I understood. He was obsessing over our English teacher, Ms. Greene. I didn't approve of his new, fucked-up fascination, but I'd never say a word about it to him. Dean, on the other hand? I had no idea what his problem was. Why hadn't he grabbed an ass and sprung into action like he normally did.

"Dean, dude, where's your piece of pussy for the night?" Trent echoed my thoughts, scrolling his thumb over the wheel on his iPod, surfing his playlist, looking desperately uninterested in the chick he was fucking.

Before Dean could answer him, Trent pushed the girl on top of him away mid-thrust, patting her head gently as she tumbled onto the sofa. Her mouth was still open, half in pleasure, half in shock.

"Sorry. It ain't happening for me tonight. It's the cast." He pointed his beer bottle to his broken ankle, smiling apologetically at his fuck buddy.

Out of the four of us, Trent was the nicest.

That said all anyone needed to know about the HotHoles.

The ironic thing was, Trent had the most reason to be spiteful. He was screwed, and he knew it. There was no way he was getting a full ride to college without football. His grades sucked ass, and his parents didn't have the money to pay for their rent, let alone his education. His injury meant he was staying in SoCal and picking up some blue-collar work if he was lucky, slumming it up with the rest of his neighborhood after spending four years with us rich Todos Santos kids.

"I'm all right, man." Dean's smile was easy, but the continuous tapping of his foot was not. "Actually, I don't want you to be blindsided by something. You listening up?" He grinned nervously, straightening his posture.

Just then, the door opened behind me. Whoever came in didn't bother to knock. Everyone knew this room was off-limits. This was the HotHoles' private party space. The rules were clear. Unless invited, you didn't come in.

The girls in the room all stared in the direction of the door, but I continued smoking weed and wishing Lucia-Alicia would move the fuck away from the bar. I needed a fresh beer and wasn't in the mood for talking.

"Whoa, hi." Dean waved to the person at the door, and I swear his whole stupid body smiled.

Jaime nodded a curt hello, tensing up in his seat and sending me a look I was too stoned to decode. Trent swiveled his head, grunting in greeting too.

"Whoever's at the door better have a fucking pizza and a pussy made of gold if they wanna stay." I clenched my teeth, finally throwing a glance over my shoulder.

"Hey, y'all."

When I heard her voice, something weird happened in my chest.

Emilia. The help's daughter. *Why is she here?* She never left the servants' apartment when I threw my parties. Plus, she hadn't glanced in my direction since she ran out of my room with her calc book last week.

"Who gave you permission to come here, Help?" I sucked my blunt, inhaled deeply and poured a cloud of rancid, sweet smoke into the air, swiveling my chair to face her.

Her azure eyes glided over me briefly before landing on someone behind me. Her lips broke into a timid grin at the sight of that person. The raucous noise of the party faded, and all I saw was her face.

"Hey, Dean." Her gaze dropped to her Vans.

Her long caramel hair was braided and flung over one of her shoulders. She had on boyfriend jeans and a *Daria* shirt deliberately mismatched with an orange wool jacket. Her sense of style was juvenile and horrid, and the back of her hand was still inked with a cherry blossom tree she'd drawn in English Lit, so why the fuck was she still hot as shit? Didn't matter. I hated her anyway. But her apparent devotion to trying not to be sexy, paired with the fact that she actually *was* sexy, always made me hard as stone.

I tore my gaze from her to Dean. He smiled back at her. A goofy smirk that begged for me to break all of his teeth.

What. The. Fuck?

"You two bumping uglies?" Jaime popped his gum, asking the question I never would've, tousling his long blond surfer hair with his fist. He didn't give two shits but knew it was something that'd interest me.

"Jesus, man." Dean got up from his seat, slapping the back of

Jaime's neck and suddenly acting like some kind of a decent guy.

I knew him too well not to recognize that he wasn't one. He'd fucked so many girls on the very sofa he'd just sat on that it was permanently imprinted with his DNA. We weren't good guys. We weren't boyfriend material, whatever the fuck that meant. Hell, we weren't even trying to hide it. And other than Jaime, who was talking crazy, plotting like a cunning freshman cheerleader to get together with Ms. Greene, we didn't do monogamy.

This—and only this—made me dislike the whole Dean and Help idea. I had enough fucking drama to deal with. I didn't want to be there when her heart broke, in my house. Shattering on *my floor*. Besides, as much as I disliked Help...she wasn't for us to destroy. She was just a country girl from Virginia with a huge smile and an annoying accent. Her personality was like a fucking Michael Bublé song. So easy and un-fucking-assuming. I mean, the girl even smiled at me when she caught me staring into her bedroom in the servants' apartment like a creep.

How stupid could a person be?

It wasn't her fault I hated her. For eavesdropping on me and Daryl all those weeks ago. For looking and sounding exactly like my stepmom, Jo.

"I'm glad you could make it. Sorry you had to come here. I didn't realize I was late. This is no place for a lady," Dean joked, grabbing his jacket from the arm of the black leather sofa and jogging to the door.

He flung his arm over her shoulder, and my left eyelid ticked.

He brushed a strand of hair that fell from her braid behind her ear, and my jaw clenched.

"Hope you're hungry. I know a really good seafood place by the marina."

She grinned. "Sure. Count me in."

He laughed, and my nostrils flared.

Then they left.

They fucking left.

I tucked the blunt back into the corner of my mouth, swiveling back to the TV. The whole room fell quiet and all eyes were directed at me for further instructions, and what the fuck was everybody so upset about?

"Hey, you." I pointed at the girl who Trent had thrown away mid-fuck. She was fixing her hair in front of the mirror next to my gaming rig. I patted my lap twice. "Over here, and bring your friend." I pinned the other one with my eyes. The girl I'd rejected only moments ago. Good thing she'd decided to stick around.

With a giggling girl on each leg, I took a hit of my joint, pulled the first girl's hair so that she was facing me and pressed my lips to hers. I exhaled, shotgunning the smoke into her mouth. She took it all in with an excited gasp.

"Move it forward." I brushed the bridge of her nose with the tip of mine, my eyes heavy. She smiled with her mouth closed and kissed the other girl on my lap, letting the smoke seep into her mouth.

Trent and Jaime watched me the whole time.

"They're probably just fuck buddies," Trent offered, rubbing his hand over his shaved head. "I didn't hear about this shit until tonight, and Dean can keep a secret like I can keep my pants up at a Playboy-mansion party."

"Yeah," Jaime chipped in. "It's Dean, dude. He's never had a serious girlfriend. He's never had a serious *anything*." Standing up, he shouldered into his navy letter jacket. "Anyway, I gotta head out."

Of course. To pretend to be some loser on a dating site and spend the night sexting Ms. Greene. I swear, if I hadn't seen his dick in the locker room, I'd assume Jaime actually had a pussy.

"But I'm telling you," he added, "don't overanalyze it. There's no way in hell Dean's settling down. He's set on New York for college. You're staying here with her. She didn't get accepted any-where, right?"

Right.

On top of that, Help hadn't bagged a scholarship so far. I knew that because we shared the same mailbox, and I browsed through her envelopes to see where little Emilia Leblanc was headed next. So far, it looked like she wasn't going anywhere, much to her dismay.

I was going to a bullshit college in Los Angeles a couple of hours away, and she was staying here. I would come back every other weekend, and she'd still be here. Catering to me.

Serving me.

Envying me.

She was going to stay small and insignificant. Uneducated and opportunity-less. And above all—*mine.*

"I really don't give a fuck." I chuckled, grabbing both the girls' asses, clutching their soft flesh as I moved them toward one another.

"Lick each other's tits for me." My tone was flat. They did as they were told. It was so easy to get them to do it, it depressed the hell out of me.

"So where were we?" I asked my friends.

The girls and their tongues were at war. They begged for my attention like two dogs fighting for their lives in an underground fight. They did nothing for me, and naturally, I resented them for that.

"In deep denial, apparently. Jesus." Jaime shook his head, sauntering to the door. He clasped Trent's shoulder on his way out. "Make sure the girls don't do anything too stupid."

"You mean like him?" Trent jerked his thumb toward me.

I squinted at him. But he didn't care. He was a kid from the hood. Nothing scared him, let alone my rich milky ass.

There was rage brimming inside me. Soon, it was going to overflow.

They were so sure they knew me. So sure I wanted Emilia LeBlanc.

"Fuck this shit. I'm going down to the pool." I stood up suddenly, and the girls collapsed, each of them landing on an arm of the chair with a soft thud.

One of them whined in protest, and the other shrieked, "What the hell!"

"Bad high," I offered as a half-assed explanation.

"It happens." The girl who'd fucked Trent a second ago smiled in understanding.

I wanted to beat the shit out of their dads almost as much as I wanted to screw up Daryl. Their availability repulsed me.

"Are you gonna call me?" Alicia-Lucia tugged on my shirt. Hope glittered in her eyes.

I gave her a slow once-over. She looked good, but not as good as she thought. Then again, she was eager to please, so probably not the worst lay.

I'd warned her.

She'd refused to listen.

And I wasn't a good guy.

"Leave your number on Trent's phone." I turned on my heel and left.

In the hallway, people made way for me, gluing their backs to the wall, smiling and raising their red Solo cups to me, groveling like I was the fucking pope. And to them—I was. This was my kingdom. People loved my type of evil. That was the thing about California, and that's why I would never leave. I loved everything other people hated about it. The liars, the pretenders, the masks, and the plastic. I loved how people cared about what was in your pocket and not in your fucking chest. I loved that they were impressed by expensive cars and cheap wit. Hell, I even loved the earthquakes and bullshit vegetable shakes.

These people who I hated were my home. This place—my playground.

Murmurs rose from every corner of the hallway. I didn't usually grace these people with my presence, but when I did, they knew why. Shit was going to go down tonight. Excitement filled the air.

"Fell in Love With a Girl" by The White Stripes pounded against the dark walls.

I didn't make eye contact with anyone. Just stared ahead as I sliced through the throng until I reached the storage cellar under the kitchen. I closed the door behind me. It was quiet, dark, like me. I pressed my back against the door, squeezed my eyes shut, and took a deep breath of the damp air.

Damn, that shit Dean brought in *was* strong. I was only half-lying when I said the stuff was bad.

I walked deeper into the room, mentally slamming the door on the rest of the world. On Daryl Ryker. Josephine. And even on people who were only half-villains, like Emilia and my dad. My fingers brushed the weapons on the wall I had collected over the years. I fingered my crowbar, dagger, baseball bat, and leather whip. It occurred to me that one day, hopefully soon, I could give up this collection, which I had never used but owned because it made me feel safer. Mainly, having this shit meant Daryl didn't mess with me anymore.

I was looking for a physical, slow-building fight. I was looking for explosive pain coming out of nowhere. In short, I was looking for trouble.

When I climbed back upstairs to the outdoor pool, empty-handed, I stood over the edge. The moonlight lit my reflection against the clear water. The pool was full of people in swim trunks and designer bikinis. My eyes roamed the place, searching for

Dean. He was the guy I wanted to fight. To break his smug boy-next-door face. But I knew he was out with Help, and besides, rules were rules. Even I couldn't bend them. The minute I stepped out there with my sleeves rolled up to my shoulders, I invited whoever wanted to fight me to step forward. But I couldn't ask anyone specifically. They had to volunteer. That was the dangerous game we played at All Saints High to burn time: *Defy*.

Defy was fair.

Defy was brutal.

Most of all, Defy dulled the pain and provided a great explanation for my marred skin.

I wasn't surprised when I heard the thump of Trent's cast behind me. He knew how fucked up I was and wanted to save the night.

"Tell Dean to dump her ass or I will," he said from behind my back.

I shook my head, sneering. "He can do whatever the fuck he wants. If he wants to bang that hillbilly, it's his funeral."

"Vicious," Trent warned.

I turned around and sized him up. His smooth mocha skin shone under the full moon, and I hated him for his ability to enjoy the opposite sex with such carelessness. Fucking random chicks was growing old too fast. And I wasn't even eighteen yet.

"This shit with this chick is gonna drag everyone down a very dark path." He took off his shirt, exposing his huge, ripped torso. He was a bulky bastard.

As always, I kept my shirt on. People eyed us avidly, but I'd never cared about these assholes. They wanted to fill their meaningless existence with something to talk about. I was only too happy to give it to them.

I coiled my fist, cocking my head sideways. "Aw, you care about me. I'm fucking touched, T-Rex." I clutched the left side of my black tee above my heart, mocking him with a fake smile.

Georgia and her airhead crew were watching us intently, waiting for the monster in me to pounce on one of my best friends. I marched past Trent, my shoulder brushing his, trudging toward the tennis court where we fought on most weekends. It was big, secluded, and spacious enough for the crowd to take seats on one side of our makeshift octagon.

"Give me your worst, Rexroth," I growled, trying to calm myself down. Trying to remind myself that Trent and Jaime were right. Dean and Help were just a fling. They'd be broken up by the end of the month. He was going to dump her—hopefully with her virginity still intact—hurt and angry and looking for a rebound. She'd be fragile, insecure, and vindictive.

And that's when I was going to strike.

That's when I was going to show her she was nothing more than my property.

"Come on, T. Move your injured ass to the tennis court. Just try not to bleed all over my fucking grass after we're done."

In the mood for another student/teacher romance? *Illicit* by Ava Harrison comes out Spring 2017. Here is a sneak-peek:

ILLICIT

Ava Harrison

PROLOGUE

Lynn

I'VE STOPPED WISHING FOR EXTRAORDINARY.

I've stopped wishing for that one moment so profound that everything will change. I know it will never happen, so there's no point in dreaming.

But like all things in life, extraordinary happens when you least expect it, and in the blink of an eye, everything can change.

CHAPTER ONE

Lynn

I GAZE OUT INTO THE vast ocean before me. The water laps against the shore like a graceful song to my ears, quietly whispering a melody I once loved, but it does nothing to calm my nerves. Waves roll in, and with each pass of the water, the sand below me scratches beneath my bare feet. I close my eyes to take in the peace, but the visions behind my eyes are still there, and the pain of his betrayal continues to etch away at me.

As usual, nothing has gone according to my plan. I'm not sure what I expected, but it certainly wasn't what I got. I've never really liked him.

So why did it hurt so much?

Life has taught me hard lessons. I learned long ago that I could never rely on anyone to be there for me, but even after everything I've been through, I still need to know I mean something to someone. That someone out there cares.

It certainly isn't my parents. My father left when I was ten, and my mom . . . well, my mom is currently in the midst of becoming Mrs. Someone for the fourth time. I'm her perfectly created specimen. The daughter she flaunts at the parties she attends.

When I was eleven, mom was trying to land a British duke, which required extensive travel to Europe, and also required me accompanying her on the many trips abroad. To this day, I'm not sure why she dragged me along. In the end, all we had to show for the experience was my being held back a grade. So, even though I'm already eighteen, I'm still only a senior in high school.

Turning my head to look over my shoulder, I gaze at the house in the distance. Right up the beach is the house party we decided to crash. Bridget's older sister rented it with a bunch of her college buddies, including my boyfriend, Matthew. Well, I guess ex-boyfriend now.

Bridget and I had decided at the last minute to pack a bag and crash the party. Although everyone at the party was significantly older then us, we knew we'd be welcomed to party with them. It would be everyone's last hurrah. I couldn't wait to get there and spend some time with Matt before school started, but it turned out he wasn't missing me as much as I missed him.

My feet were cemented to the floor as I took in the sight before me. There, standing at the edge of the bed, was my boyfriend and a blonde I don't know. I couldn't move as I watched him thrust in and out of her from behind. The sickly sweet smell of sex permeated through the room.

I was afraid I'd be sick.

"Matt."

"Oh, shit," he said as he pulled out of her and faced me. "Fuck. I didn't know you'd be here."

"You didn't know I would be here?"

He made no move to cover himself or his whore. Instead, I was forced to look at the woman he cheated on me with. Model tall with bones sticking out of her hips—the complete opposite of me. Her hair was the shade of blonde only present in a bottle and she had lips that looked as if they had recently been injected with fillers. Shaking my head, I turned my attention back to Matt whose dick was still hard and mouth hung open, obviously thinking of a way to respond to my question. He let out an audible sigh and then—finally—reached for a sheet to cover the evidence of his tryst.

"Listen, Lynn. I'm sorry you found out this way, but maybe it's for the best."

My stomach tightened, and anger coiled inside me. "For the best? What the fuck, Matt? We've been together for months!"

"Yeah, but I'm going away to college, and I'm not sure how I can go that long without you. I have needs."

"Needs? You know what? No. No! You don't get to put this on me like it's my fault you're a lying, cheating dick. I'm out of here. Have a nice life."

"Lynn—"

I stormed out the door.

I take a deep breath and the smell of the ocean rushes up through my nose. It's salty and pungent fragrance should act as a balm, an elixir that soothes me, but I'm too destroyed for something that simple to work. I exhale the emotion collecting inside me.

All I can do now is pray for a miracle to save my night.

By Ava Harrison

Imperfect Truth
Through Her Eyes
trans·fer·ence

About the Author

Ava Harrison is a New Yorker, born and bred. When she's not journaling her life, you can find her window shopping, cooking dinner for her family, or curled up on her couch reading a book.

Website: avaharrisonauthor.com
Facebook: on.fb.me/1E9khDv
Twitter @avaharrison333
Instagram @AvaHarrisonAuthor
Pinterest bit.ly/1Qo0Tw1

Printed in Great Britain
by Amazon